ACCLAIM FOR

For Those Who Hunt the W

"Invested with a passion and acuity that
of smug misunderstanding and ideologica
David Adams Richards writes novels that are essential. . . ."
— *Canadian Forum*

"Richards is a writer of great talent and mighty vision. In Richards' marvelous characters . . . we see ourselves."
— *Telegraph Journal*

"A distillation of powerful feeling, and an eloquent call for compassion. . . . A remarkable book."
— *Quill & Quire* (starred review)

"Compelling. . . . The fire in Richards' voice makes the action explosive. . . ."
— *Edmonton Journal*

"This novel is powerful: a wrenching subject is developed with skill and sensitivity. Richards has created a place for Jerry Bines in the pantheon of twentieth-century tragic heroes."
— *Calgary Herald*

"His writing seems to reflect the unflinching nature of man. . . . He masterfully mixes tension and fear with a poignancy that is itself wounding."
— Halifax *Daily News*

"Richards wants us to avoid easy explanations, the ones that separate us from 'the wounded' and just explain them away."
— Kingston *Whig-Standard*

"Richards is a painfully sharp observer, who possesses one of the most distinct and compelling voices in contemporary literature."
— *Toronto Star*

FOR THOSE WHO HUNT
THE WOUNDED DOWN

DAVID ADAMS RICHARDS

M&S

Canadian Cataloguing in Publication Data

Richards, David Adams, 1950–
For those who hunt the wounded down : a novel

ISBN 0-7710-7515-4

I. Title.

PS8585.I17F6 2001   C813´.54   C93-094130-6
PR9199.3.R42F6 2001

For her help, the author wishes to thank his editor, Ellen Seligman.

We acknowledge the financial support of the Government of
Canada through the Book Publishing Industry Development
Program for our publishing activities.

We further acknowledge the support of the Canada Council for the
Arts and the Ontario Arts Council for our publishing program.

Cover design: Ingrid Paulson
Cover image: Brad Wilson/Photonica

Printed and bound in Canada

McClelland & Stewart Ltd.
The Canadian Publishers
481 University Avenue
Toronto, Ontario
M5G 2E9
www.mcclelland.com

1 2 3 4 5   04 03 02 01 00

"The rifle kicks hard both ways."

Eric Trethewey
(from "Killing Whiskey")

In 1981, during the interval between AA speakers at the meeting in the prison, a man was led in late. He was placed at the back of the crowded room.

It was an AA meeting that Joe Walsh chaired every week here because he felt he was duty-bound to do it.

But the man they had brought in that evening, who sat looking around cautiously, and at the same time impervious to other prisoners, was Joe's nephew, Jerry Bines.

So after the meeting, feeling compelled that he should speak, Joe walked over to him. But it was Jerry who broke the ice.

"How are you, Joe," he said. "Doin good – doing

good right – drivin tractor-trailer now – that's what being sober will get you."

"Yes," Joe answered. And he could not help but smile, because of how Jerry's face lit up when he saw him.

"Good – good –"

He thanked Joe for coming, and said that he would start to attend these meetings on a regular basis now.

"You like them."

"Don't like them, no – no don't like them – gives me a chance to get out a my cell – out of my cell," Jerry said, smiling.

Then he asked about Joe's family. And then he paused, as if trying to think of something to say.

"Your daughter Adele's got herself a good lad now," Jerry said innocently. "Ralphie Pillar, right – I like Adele – always have," he said. "When I first went to Kingsclear – she was the only one to write – only one." He glanced away when he said this as if thinking of something. . . . "Don't blame those who didn't," he said.

"How long are you here for?" Joe said.

"Christ, I don't know – three or four years or so," Jerry said, and he looked around as if musing at this. "Three years – and then I'll be free." He stood up to go.

Joe remembered Jerry's father and his mother as he watched him go, and he wanted to say something kind, but, as always with Joe, words failed him. He only watched his nephew who, even when he moved in shackles, reminded Joe of himself.

A few years passed.

And the town grew up around them and became another town. And they grew older.

When Jerry got out of prison, he was twenty-three. He married a young woman from Lyttleton and had a son, who he called William Digger Bines, after his father. His past seemed to be gone, and often he attended AA meetings that Joe went to at the small schoolroom up on the highway. He wouldn't speak himself, and at the end of the night he would have a coffee in a styrofoam cup, before he left, alone. Now and then he would glance at someone coming in, or someone leaving whom he perhaps had confrontations with in his past, but he wouldn't say anything.

Joe helped Jerry and his wife out with money, and Jerry worked the boats. His wife, they said, was small and attractive and fervently religious – and this is what happened to him (that is, the hope of change through the celebration of a positive female character).

You would see him standing beside Joe at AA meetings or passing alone through darkness along the street.

"That's Jerry Bines," someone would whisper.

"Oh – I always wanted to know what he looked like," someone else would say.

"Well, there he is – see, see, there he is."

He occasionally sat with Joe's wife Rita at night, reminiscing. That is, Jerry would mostly listen to stories she knew about his mother and father, the dances they went to, when they were all firebrands of a sort and smouldering young.

Joe had brought a new kind of chair for Rita to rest upon because she was sick, and Jerry would sit across from her as she spoke with her head slanted down to the left. He would nod at her quietly as she spoke in the dark, the spring air through the opened windows smelling of soft earth and paint, the town chugging silently into the future. Jerry was always polite and respectful to everyone. Joe and Rita never had very much – and Jerry knew this. Rita and Joe had taken care of him after his own mother's death in 1968.

Now and then when he wasn't working a boat Jerry went with Joe on his tractor-trailer runs. Joe never really knew how Jerry was doing, because Jerry would touch Joe's shoulder – a touch that by its very nature or the nature of the toucher seemed more compassionate than an ordinary man's: "Good, Joe – doin good – don't worry about me."

His smile too was so infectious that it was like a lamp going on. How was this?

Joe talked incessantly about his son-in-law, Ralphie Pillar, about how intelligent and kindly he was, and Jerry seemed particularly interested in him.

"I could never do that," Jerry mumbled one day when speaking about Ralphie being hired as a consultant for a government study. "All them brains – some smart, eh?"

But he seemed embarrassed to say this, as if it were a

4

world he did not understand.

"Like Adele too – always did –"

And Joe felt sad that he had bragged a little.

§

In the summer of 1986 Joe's tractor-trailer was stolen and a month later Jerry was charged with the murder of Buddy Savoie, in a dispute at the Savoie house. No one could prove he was implicated in the tractor-trailer hijacking. No one could prove it was murder either, or that the gun would actually fire twice in succession, which seemed to prove Jerry's testimony that Buddy had a knife and so he had picked up the gun as a last resort.

And he was acquitted because of this.

But his wife and son left him because of his terrible past, and he no longer took in the meetings.

Rita often talked about him. But she was not able to see him, and she died before he went to trial.

Adele no longer wanted anything to do with him, though she had heard that Jerry still spoke fondly of her and of Ralphie. She knew too that she could contact him in a moment if need be. And that he would come.

But he was, in fact, a part of the family that no one mentioned. Adele did not mention him to Ralphie, thinking that they would never meet.

Again a year passed. Joe Walsh died as broke as he had been most of his life, attending meetings to

5

stay sober and never once saying anything against Jerry
Bines.

By 1989 Jerry began to be seen again in town.

1

The boy Andrew met him in a hunting camp. He was ordinary in every way except for his eyes, and the small scar above one of them. He had a tattoo of a star between his thumb and forefinger and he wore a parka and toque.

If he was down on his luck he didn't say so. He had a peculiar way of expression; almost everything seemed to be said slowly and in duplicate. "That's no good – no good," he would say. Or if asked how he was he would reply. "Not too bad – too bad – how are you?"

And he would smile. He had a wonderfully attractive smile, a smile which suggested that he would die in a second for whatever he believed in, in whatever place, no matter what.

And so the boy, who was only nine, was drawn to this quality, as boys generally are, infatuated with it, as boys generally are, and romanticized this man immediately as being the kind of man he would like to be himself. It was because of the object of his look, the almost casual disregard for private benefit when he spoke to others.

"He was the only man to ever come over the wall at Dorchester," someone mentioned.

He did not stay long. His camp was further away and he'd only come in here to see how they were making out.

Then he left.

"Do you know who he is?" someone said, a man at the camp who liked to think he knew people very well, and could tell others about them.

"He's Jerry Bines," the man said. "Have you ever heard of him?"

"No," the boy said.

"Well, you will," the man answered him, smiling delightedly at himself. "You will. Jerry Bines," he said. "You have to stay away from lads like that."

He said that Bines was down on his luck. His little boy had leukemia.

And so the conversation went back and forth from one man to the other as they sat in the smoke-filled gloomy camp, and the boy sat on the edge of the chair listening. Fog rolled in between the thick dark spruces and the lane was muddy and dotted with puddles as far as the eye could see.

The boy was generally kept away from all of this conversation in any other locale; but because he was in the camp with men there was a certain idea that he was of age. The talk was not disturbing to him, except for one thing which none of the men knew. He thought of how sad it must be to be *outside* of life, and that Jerry's physical aspects took on a certain heaviness, as if the physical space he inhabited was somehow different and more limited than that of the other men there. He did not know how to articulate this, of course, and perhaps this feeling came because he was young and not given to all the froth and worry of the men themselves.

As the afternoon wore on they spoke about Bines' father and how he had a plate in his head from the Korean war.

"Did he really take Jerry out to fight other boys in the pulpyards for a quart of wine?" one man said.

"I heard that," the man spoke, as if nothing was unknown or surprising to him, and that this had happened was a certainty which he delighted in.

"But that's the worst thing I ever heard of," another said. "That's the most terrible thing I ever heard of," he added lowly, keeping at bay all of his anger — as if getting angry at anything associated with Bines was not the thing to do, even when the man was not present.

But the man said it wasn't the most terrible thing, and he related how other men had acted with their children. "Making them become priests or professors," he said. "Or, worse still, lawyers."

The young boy sat there in the gloom listening. He thought of his own father who had died, and who had loved him, and of his uncle whom he now lived with.

He too was an orphan, in a way – like Bines was – but how different their lives. Learning his catechism at Sunday school, and learning about the crucifixion, he was told that each drop of blood Christ had shed was shed for a particular sin. This perhaps exaggerated claim was now manifested in the boy's psyche when he thought of Bines, whom he had witnessed walking into the gloom of the trees and looking back over his left shoulder and then becoming a spot in the globes of fog that seemed to surface from the road. He thought of a drop of blood for Bines' look, and another for a murder, and imagined as he did a picture of Christ in his small catechism.

He thought of his priest, his white soutane, his bowing when he took the host, and saying: "Body of Christ."

And all of these memories and impressions came flooding in upon him when they spoke. Perhaps no one else thought of them. But he himself was only a child and therefore could think of these things without self-recrimination.

An argument of sorts started in the camp over the severity of Bines' actions in comparison with other men who led respectable lives. It was, of course, the ageless argument.

The men spoke differently after Bines left. When he

was present they, all of them, directed their conversation to him, and he politely listened.

"Don't know about that," he would say. "Don't know." Or "Ya – that's right – right, ya."

But when he was gone, they mocked their own fear of him, and their voices rose perceptibly as if to thwart some feeling of former intimidation, which they only secretly admitted in the privacy of their hearts.

The boy noticed this but disregarded it and forgave it in a second as he was always forced to do with adults, not because he was so humble, but because he now understood their psychology.

As the evening came on he imagined Bines in his camp alone.

"He spends all his time alone now – he hardly sees his wife and little boy."

That was because of the shooting of Buddy Savoie in 1986, the first man maintained.

"It wasn't the first man he shot," someone else said.

"Well, no one knows. He did enough, though – enough."

"Did enough to last two lifetimes."

The boy himself wanted to fly an airplane. He had airplanes all over his bedroom. And if he could do this, he wouldn't want to do anything else. He thought that he would fly his mother everywhere she went.

"No one knows what happened between him and Buddy – except Buddy tried to kill him and so he was forced to defend himself."

"Well, that's what they say anyway."

"Buddy shot though the walls of his house at him – with his wife and baby boy there – the night before."

Then the conversation turned to the moose they should be able to get in the morning, if by good fortune it turned colder. Bines had told them, in fact, where there were moose, and each one of the men was now anticipating this.

As the wind came up the boy snuggled into his sleeping bag, on a bed at the back of the room behind the stairwell. It would grow colder tonight and the fog would lift. In fact, after a while it started to clear and a large moon came out and shone down upon the mud that was already half-frozen.

Late at night the boy woke as a truck went by, casting a feeble yellow light against the walls of this strange place.

Two weeks passed. It was now early October, 1989.

The sky was growing dark and he came out at the edge of the chopdown, back from this place on the river about one-third of a mile. The wind was from the north and the sun was at the trees, beginning to set. The moon seemed to be sitting directly upon it, in the darkening, bleeding twilight. Far away he could hear a pulp truck rattle and throttle out one of the logging roads a mile or more away. The highway below, soundless without a car, stretched broken and cold, between small white houses and propped barns, into the distance until he lost sight of it at the top of a faraway hill.

Now that he knew where he was – he had been mixed up for a time this last hour – he turned swiftly and went back into the trees again, so anyone standing far away on one of the chopdowns – many gorged and pitiless humps of soil and torn, thrashed roots – would have believed he was an apparition at the edge of the cedar swamp.

He was not seen in the open again until after dark. Then a man crossed the main road at a place between two smaller woods roads, between the mature spruce of two woodlots some miles from the chopdown, and disappeared again.

A half-hour later he was at his destination. He sat in the field of dry deadened hay and looked down towards the house with its one upstairs light on. He could see her moving back and forth in the window, in the space between a twisted hanging curtain.

He moved slowly towards the door and knocked lightly and entered.

He nodded to her. "How's William," he said.

His son had just come from the hospital. There was something the matter again.

Bines sat down at the wooden table and looked at her.

"He has another appointment," she said.

His wife had left him and had taken the boy. He didn't mind any more. And he knew what was going to happen now, and, because of this, he had come to ask his wife a favour: "I think we should change his name."

"To what?"

"To your name – your name – it'd be better for the boy – better for William."

"Well, everyone on the river knows who he is."

"No, no – better for the boy – better for the boy," he said. "Better for the boy," he added again, staring through her.

He didn't like this but he couldn't think of what else to do at the moment.

"I'll have to go to a lawyer to get the name changed – it's a lot of rigamarole."

"Lot of rigamarole, ya – lot of rigamarole," Bines said as if reflecting on something else.

She told him that the doctors had made him another appointment for a blood analysis.

"We could take him down to Halifax now – down there ourselves," he said, suddenly. "We could – take him down there – take him down there," he said.

"Well – the appointment's set. I think if we went and prayed at the church for him," his wife said. She was a Pentecostal girl and although she would do whatever she could for her son she didn't put as much faith in specialists as others.

"Ya, well – anyway – you go," he said. "That's all right – you go."

He went in to see his boy. He was four years old but he looked younger. He had not gained much weight and Bines stood over him for a moment, looking at this small face turned sideways against his teddy bear. His face had a white pallor, his lips slightly blue.

"How ya doin?" Bines said to the sleeping boy. "How ya doing, boy?" He went to touch his head – but Bines had hardly ever touched his son, and his large hand only slightly touched the pillow.

"I might burn my house," Bines said when he came back out.

His wife looked at him.

"My camp too," Bines said. "People coming to get even for the tractor-trailer racket. Gary Percy's on his way back. They let him out on day parole and he's gone."

His wife didn't answer. But the fear she'd always secretly held for him took sway. He looked at her.

"Don't worry about it – I'll straighten things around – get a sprocket for the bicycle for him – you wait and see."

After giving his wife some money – and after telling her she would have to make do for a while on her own – he turned at the door to look at her, and then towards the room where Willie slept. After he left his wife he crossed the river, at the farthest point of the bend.

Jerry Bines' father had shot through his bedroom wall in an attempt to commit suicide when Jerry was fourteen.

"I hit the floor that fuckin time," Jerry would say.

The only thing his father left was a house at the end of a dirt road. The only thing he gave Jerry was a watch with a studded strap, which Jerry now wore. He had cancer in his stomach and wouldn't go to the hospital, and Jerry used to go out and buy him Aspirin and Rolaids and come home and force his mouth open.

"Here ya go now – here ya go," he would say as his father sat on his bed, the sheet covered with sweat. "Here ya go," Jerry said.

Jerry had loved his mother but she had died when he was four years old. She was Joe Walsh's sister, and he had always liked Adele and her younger sister Milly, though they wouldn't speak to him after he was fifteen.

Jerry was Dr. Hennessey's namesake and godchild. The night he was born a storm had closed the roads and schools and made travel impossible. His father had hitched the old horse and put his mother on the sleigh and started down the river, beating the horse around the ears to get it across the ice.

And when they came up over the bank near the bridge Hennessey was waiting for them. He had come out as far as the bridge but couldn't make it past. The horse's face was turned against the storm and capped with snow, and seemed eerie in the lights of the tractor-trailer that was trying to secure passage.

When he was little he used to sing for the men who visited the house: songs like "love's going to live here – love's going to live here – love's going to live here again" and "the lights – in the harbour – they don't shine for me – I'm like a lost ship – adrift in the sea – sea of heart-break, lost loves, and loneliness."

And walk three miles to get a pop at the corner store.

You turn right instead of left and your life changes forever without your knowing any change has come. Or you need a sprocket for a child's bike and turn in one direction instead of another.

One afternoon Ralphie Pillar was working in his shop. When he looked up, a man was standing with his back to him looking out the window at the dusty gravel lot turning to hard callused dirt in the afternoon sun.

The man was caught in this afternoon sun, this October afternoon drawing to a close. (Ralphie looking at him was suddenly reminded of things far away and almost forgotten.) His back appeared to be a part of the wall, near the window where he stood. The window trembled slightly in the wind – a few leaves blew upwards in the yard and became still again while the sun made an effort to regain the cloud.

Suddenly the man looked over and smiled, sunlight on his cheek. Far away in the great afternoon children scrambled and kicked the drywall boards of an old building. It was Thanksgiving weekend.

"Hello, Ralphie," the man said, as if he'd always known him.

Ralphie nodded and smiled, but he wasn't quite sure who the man was. There was something instantly unapproachable about him, though, even when he turned and smiled. And Ralphie instinctively wanted to draw away. Ralphie had become a quiet, reflective man and he didn't know many people in town anymore.

But then he realized, after a moment or two, that it was Jerry Bines.

Bines' smile, however, seemed nothing but kind and even wonderful.

Ralphie was tall and thin, with delicate facial features, but he had deceived himself into thinking he was much taller, for when Bines walked up to him he was almost as tall, but far more powerful when he held Ralphie's hand and pressed it in his own.

"I wonder if ya got one of these," he said. And he hauled out a small sprocket for a bicycle.

Ralphie said he didn't have one in his shop but he would look around, and for Bines to come back.

At first he didn't think anything about this, but after Bines left Ralphie had the strangest sensation, just as the sun came in on the old yellow window plant, of a kind of euphoria that Bines would bother to ask him this favour.

He did not know initially why he had this feeling. But, of course, it all had to do with Bines being famous and wild.

That night he told Adele about meeting him. He spoke of the way he looked when he was inside the door.

And again he was pleased, as if he had been filled with a kind of grace, and this made him agitated.

"He's my cousin," she said.

"What do you mean?"

"C-O-U-S-I-N." She spelled it out. And then sniffed.

Ralphie was silent. It was Thanksgiving. Joe and Rita were both gone, and so too was Ralphie's mother, Thelma. All had died within the space of six years. Though Ralphie was in his thirties, his hair was now turning whiter, his face was even thinner than it had been.

"Stay away from him, Ralphie-face – he's bad news."

"Oh, he just wants a sprocket," Ralphie said. "What do you mean, your cousin?"

"We are cousins – me, Milly, he – cousins. He's the bad side of the family – you'd do no good to broker pleasantries with him," she said in the old-fashioned way.

Ralphie laughed. "I thought you were the bad side of the family," he said.

"Not a little bit," she glanced up at him quickly. "Joe tried to get him settled down for two years – took him to AA, helped find him a job – but all as it did was cost Joe his life. Who do you think set up the tractor-trailer?"

"Oh – I don't believe that," Ralphie said, suddenly angrier than he should be for some reason, and reflecting on how kind Bines seemed to be to him.

"I have no use for him, Ralphie," she said.

"Well, either do I," Ralphie said, annoyed. And decided not to mention Bines again.

He actually did find a sprocket in his box of spare parts. And Bines did come back the next afternoon.

"How much?" Jerry asked.

"Oh, nothing," Ralphie said, "I'd never use it, never miss it – go ahead."

"Well, I'll do you a favour then some day," Bines said. "Do you a favour."

The little boy had come to Adele and asked her to tie his shoe, and stood there weaving as small boys do.

He was her cousin from upriver and his mother was sick. They had brought her to the hospital the day before because she wouldn't stop bleeding, and now he was getting ready to go to visit her.

His father was Digger Bines, and he had already made a fuss at the hospital and had hit the priest.

Adele, who was seven, did not tell him this. But the boy still sensed that things were not right and he kept staring at his Aunt Rita as if to get her to explain something. It was as if this was his first glimpse of the darker world, and he was perplexed.

His name was Jerry Bines, and that was Adele's first memory of him, tying his shoe in the May sunshine, and Jerry standing above her talking about worms and fishing and red spinners.

He had talked nonstop about visiting his mother, and he had bolt-black, almost contagiously brave eyes that could stare at you for an hour without so much as a

20

blink. And he would not stand still when they fussed with his suit, which seemed to be a patchwork job of two or three suits, and a pair of brown shoes, second or third hand, which were two sizes too large, so Rita had stuffed newspaper in the toes. He ran upstairs to get the new pin for his lapel.

Jerry wanted to tell everyone that Adele was his girlfriend, but he said he would only tell his mother.

Adele remembered something else. Digger bought Jerry a huge family-pack size of potato chips that morning and he carried them wherever he went, offering them to everyone as if he was the richest boy in the world. Also, he was very excited because he was going to take a taxi.

He placed the chip bag carefully on top of his suitcase when he ran to get into the taxi to go and visit his mom, and stuck his feet out the window one at a time. "New shoes," he said seriously to passersby, being driven with his half-mad father up the lane, "new shoes."

People turned on the sidewalk to watch and Jerry fell back against the seat, while everything in the world was in bloom.

When his mother died the next afternoon, Adele sat at the table with him, and, putting her arm around him said, "I'm your forever girlfriend." And she smiled.

All of this had been forgotten and swept away, down a thousand other avenues and years, until now.

2

Bines was already famous. People had heard a great deal about him. So it was not an unusual request that Ralphie's sister Vera had to meet him and to write his story. She had gone to Adele for her help. Vera now worked for the department of social services, specializing in child welfare. She had divorced her husband Nevin for mental and emotional cruelty, and spoke calmly about this, and about her refusal to let Nevin see their child, Hadley.

It wasn't that his story interested her so much. But he fitted a pattern that she had concerned herself about over the last four or five years. And she had convinced herself that she could expose this pattern better than anyone else, show his kind of male violence, show the broader scope of such violence and how it "impacted" on children and women. "Impacted" being the new word of choice for her at this moment.

He was going to be one of the many people she would write about, but she felt that he would be at the centre of a long history of "maleness" and "patriarchy," which is how she described it, to her friends and devotees.

She felt that she too would become famous with this book, at least in a small way amongst a certain group.

Vera was now in her forties. Her hair was short. She was too tall for her weight. She had done some freelance work for magazines and she had travelled.

And it seemed to her at the moment that Jerry Bines was the personification of her concern. And she felt this because he had become famous. She went to see Adele after Thanksgiving.

"Why do you come to me for this?" Adele said.

"Well, first of all he's your cousin."

"That doesn't matter – I don't like him."

"Well, like doesn't matter. No one says we should like him. In fact it's probably preferable not to like him."

Adele thought this over for a second. *Why did I ever get mixed up with the Pillar family – it's just a family-pack of loons.*

Adele did not like this idea. It seemed to her to be like every other idea Vera had. And on the other side there was something cheating about not liking him if you were going to use him.

"If you don't like him, why would you bother to want to do a book on him?" Adele said.

"Would he let me do a book on him?" Vera said.

"Why would he want you to write anything about him if you don't like him – and why would you want to?"

But again Vera said that like or not like did not matter. She would be fair and objective, and that was more important.

Like or not like meant very much to Adele, however. Nothing else ever mattered more. And there were a good deal of things she would not tell anyone about Jerry. She gave a sigh.

That Vera would come to Adele, whom she never had liked, made her suddenly seem vulnerable, however. And this is what made Adele feel sorry for her. A book to Adele was nothing. There were too many of them around anyway – just heaps of them – and now Vera wanted to write one. Just as Adele had predicted she would.

"Are you scared of him?" Vera said. She had her tape-recorder going and Adele glanced at it suspiciously.

"Am I being interviewed or something like that?" Adele said.

"No, no – this won't be used."

"I'd be a fool not to be scared of him," Adele said, "and so would anyone else – but we both have something in common."

"Oh, what's that?" Vera said.

"We're both exceptionally good haters – and neither of us has ever forgotten a kindness or an insult."

"My," Vera said. "Dear, dear, dear."

Adele shifted her gaze and looked about.

"What I'm saying is – if you use him, use him right." But again she was angry. She herself did not want to use Bines rightly or wrongly. She knew too many things that she couldn't say.

"Will I be frightened of him?" Vera said.

"Only if he wants you to be," Adele said. Then she sighed.

"He's the kind of man who if he can't beat you with his fist would get a brick."

"Well, this is just what I'm after," Vera said delightedly. And her severe brushed hair seemed suddenly to testify to this.

"He's been in prison four times, he's been involved," Adele said. "And he has people who would kill him like that." She snapped her fingers. "If they weren't scared to death to."

"That's just what I want," Vera said again. "I want all of that."

Of all the lost and hopeless why did her cousin become famous. And why was this happening? Ralphie and she were finally content. They had given up their only child, a daughter, which was the worst thing they had ever done. But nothing could be done about it now. They had talked themselves into it and regretted it instantly and forever.

They had their own home and their own lives. And though Adele could not have another child they had resigned themselves to it.

"So when can I see him?" Vera said.

The meeting was arranged for two nights later.

All day long Adele sat in the huge wicker chair in the back room staring out of the huge old windows at her trampled little garden, which had grown nothing but a few radishes and some brown tomatoes. It seemed a mistake to get mixed up in things best forgotten and so ultimately dangerous.

By 5:00 the dusk came and made her go back into the kitchen.

"Don't they know what they are getting themselves in for?" Adele said, lighting a cigarette – her first in three weeks – and feeling abysmal because she had lighted it.

Of course she knew all about Bines and they did not, and she could not tell them – because her family had refused to speak about him, and so she had refused too. But still there was another reason. Once Bines came into the room he could command them to like him. He had always been able to, and she was frightened of this. It was not a sexual attraction, more a kind of devotion. And it was this devotion she had already seen in Ralphie, who knew nothing about him.

At 7:00 Vera arrived.

"Is he here yet?" Vera said.

"No – perhaps he won't come –"

The three of them sat in the small parlour off the living room.

Every now and again Ralphie would stretch his long legs out and then bring them back, smile, and then bend forward, as if trying his best to find something to do.

At quarter to eight the small clock in the hallway gonged, and Vera stood and walked into the living room.

"He won't be here," Adele said.

She watched Vera pace back and forth for a minute, and then come in through the dark hallway to the parlour again.

"Well, maybe he's frightened to come," Vera said.

"No – he's right behind you," Adele answered.

Vera turned her head, gave a startled jump, and moved more quickly along the hall.

"Give ya a start – a start, did I?" Bines said.

His voice was extremely soft, almost indescribably so, yet it had an unusual expansive quality to it. And it had with it, in its intonation, a completely uncomplicated River accent.

The first thing that was apparent to them was that Bines was reluctant to go anywhere now. He came late and said he only had a moment.

When he walked in, the house was almost dark, yet a

soft light glowed from the lamp in the room and Vera had set up her tape-recorder. As he came from the darkness into the light Adele remembered that she had not really seen him in a long while.

He looked so much like her cousins from that other side of the family – the darker side, which Joe and Rita had always tried to protect the children from. He looked, for instance, like their cousin Packet Terri – except he was slighter. Adele felt strange that he was in her house, because she immediately felt that she must do something for him. And this was exactly the kind of devotion that he inspired.

Jerry shook Vera's hand like a man who was so unused to this common civility that it embarrassed him, and then he smiled.

"Ralphie's sister – right," he said.

He said this not to make sure that he had gotten the relationship right but to show that he would treat her with the respect that Ralphie's sister accorded.

And then he sat down on the small couch directly across from Adele. Adele tried everything not to look towards him but it was impossible.

"Hello, Delly," he said quietly, after watching her for a moment.

When she looked up at him he winked. In a way this was done to bring her closer to him, in an instant.

"Sorry to hear about Joe," he said softly. "Joe – always liked Joe – always liked Joe. He come to jail all the time – all the time when I was there. Try to straighten us around. I didn't know his heart was bad – bad there – like your mom's too."

Adele only nodded at this, and then gave a sigh as if she was about to say something but thought better of it.

Vera then explained the nature of her request. It would be done only if he wanted to, and in the way he wanted it done.

"Write an article on me – why would no one want to do that?" he said.

He spoke with his head slightly slanted to the right.

"Oh, but you're just the person I want to do it on," Vera said. "Everyone's heard so much about you."

"About me – ya – about me," he said. He glanced at Ralphie as if he were wondering about something, perhaps wondering who was telling things about him, and then he shrugged.

There was a long silence as he looked at them. All of them felt uncomfortable, and even frightened. But to him it was just a casual stare.

"Get Jerry a beer," Adele said to Ralphie.

Jerry glanced sideways at Ralphie a second and then looked away, as if he were puzzled.

"Article – ya – don't matter none to me."

"It will only take a week or so – maybe two," Vera said. "And then, after the transcript is done, you can read it."

"Then it better not have any big words on it – cause I don't read so good," Jerry said softly, and he smiled.

But when she went to turn on the recorder, he said, "No – not now – some other place – other place – I'll go to your place."

"When," Vera said, disappointed.

"Oh, I'll go over in a week or two – week or two," he said.

"I'll give you my address then, and phone," Vera said.

"No, no – I know where you live," he said.

Then he told them he couldn't stay. That his young lad was back in the hospital for his blood test and he wanted to go over.

"You have a child," Vera said, "that's right."

"Little boy is sick – little boy who's sick," Jerry said. "What's he got –?"

Adele looked at him a moment, startled. It was not that he did not know – it was that he was struggling with the word.

"Leukemia," Adele said, kindly.

"Ya – got that," Jerry said. "Lots of children got that – I guess – nowadays." And then he said, as if he had calculated an advantage by saying it, "It's what they put in our water now on the river – right, Ralphie?"

Ralphie, known as a conservationist, blushed, for some reason, and nodded, and Jerry nodded too.

Then he stood, said goodbye, and seemed to move away as silently as he had come.

"So that's Mr. Jerry Bines," Vera said, as a person does when someone is brought for their benefit to study.

"That's him," Adele said.

And she picked up another cigarette and lit it, and puffed out her cheeks.

In so many ways Bines was familiar to her. The problem was, as she told Ralphie that night, that once he thought you liked him he would like you – in fact he would die for you in a second, but then you could never not like him.

"Oh, don't be ridiculous," Ralphie said. "I'll never see him again – I don't even know if he'll go to see Vera. I know one thing: he's not worth worrying about."

Adele said nothing more. She sat on the side of the bed, scratching at her feet. The moon was pale over the old trampled garden, and below them on the street some rocks shone yellow in the night. It was fall and the house smelled of dry paint. It was a house they had moved into two years before.

After Ralphie turned off the lights everything in the house was still, except the *tick-tock* of the clock downstairs in the hall.

It was as if nothing had ever happened to disrupt their lives.

"I feel sorry for his little boy," Ralphie said, whispering in the dark.

"Do you ever see Nevin any more, Ralphie-face?"

"Not since I had to throw him out of my shop for whining about Vera," Ralphie said, almost asleep. "Anyway, I'll go over tomorrow and see him again."

"Vera won't try to use Bines, will she? I mean not for her own sake."

"No, no –"

"Because he won't like it if she does. He'll give her all the benefit of the doubt, but if she tricks him –"

There was a pause, and Adele turned to face him. He could see in the light from the street her small nose covered in cream.

"I don't like this," she said.

"Why not?"

She paused and then sighed, and her voice was cold when she spoke.

"Something is going on – it's time on this river for something to happen once again."

§

Jerry actually went to Vera's house four nights later. When he came in she was aware of how uncomfortable she was with him at first.

But he didn't seem to notice this. He smiled at Hadley, her little girl.

"Nice dress ya got there – nice dress. What's that, yer dolly – got a doll, do ya?"

He looked up at Vera and smiled as he just lightly touched the top of the girl's head.

"She's having some small trouble with her father," Vera whispered (intimating that this was a natural thing

for children to have). "He was just here." And then smiling suddenly, she said: "Anyway, everything will go better sooner than we think. Won't it, Hadley? There will be
no more emotional violence." And she touched Hadley's
head in a devotional way, brushing Bines' hand as she
did. Hadley looked as if this kind of thing had been
going on a long time.

Bines nodded at them both.

"That's good then – that's good," he said, though for
some peculiar reason he did not like the little girl.

Vera now wanted to do the interview in three stages.
Which would mean more than three meetings. One of
the problems she faced was that she had heard so many
stories about him.

After getting Bines to talk, at one point she interrupted him rudely, saying: "Well, that can't be right
because in 1968 your mother died and you went to live
with Joe Walsh's family – so perhaps you were too young
to remember."

Bines looked at her a moment.

"I remember what I say – remember what I say," he
said, and, flicking his hand up towards his eye, as if he
was distracted, he continued speaking. "Anyway, my
father took care of me as best he could," he said.

"Well," Vera said, quickly, "wasn't there some problem –?"

"No problem," Bines said.

"Oh," Vera said, "I'm sorry, I thought there was more of a problem – with you and your father?"

Again Bines looked at her, puzzled, and trying to think of what she had heard, trying to find a common ground.

"All people have problems in a way – in a way," Bines said, quietly.

"But wasn't he a failed boxer – and didn't he want you to box?"

"No," Bines said.

He looked at the tape-recorder.

"Does the recorder make you uncomfortable?" she asked.

"Only when it's on," Bines said.

"Okay," Vera said quickly, "but it's best if it's on. So, in 1971, you went back to live with your dad?"

"Is this going to be in the paper?" Bines said suddenly, smiling at her.

"Part of it might be – but actually I'm doing a book. So, in 1971, you went to live with your father again?"

"In September of 1970 I went to live with my father again."

"Why did you feel you had to do this – was there pressure from him?"

"No – no pressure. He was drunk as an arse downtown sitting in front of Lounsbury's with people stepping over him. I was on my way home from school – from school and I went and helped him. I sat down by

34

him, to keep passersby from bothering him – you know, bothering him – I stayed there three hours – three hours keeping an eye on him."

"I see," Vera whispered. "Did you feel obligated to do this? I mean, why did you feel you had to?"

Bines did not understand these questions.

"Obligated – no – not so much. He was my father."

"But people said he threw you against a stove and beat you – didn't he?"

"He had a bad head on him. He sometimes couldn't help what he did."

"So even then you felt obligated to take care of him?"

"Obligated, no – no obligation." And he again moved his hand, with an unfathomable sense of power up against his right eye, as if to ward something off.

"Well," Vera said, "we can come back to that later. At any rate –"

"Come back, ya –"

"Were you treated badly at the Walshes'?"

"No – not at all – treated all right – just wasn't my home."

Again Vera wanted to bring the subject around.

"And you don't think your father was to blame – in any way? I mean for your mother's early death?"

"No – why would he be?"

Vera looked up at him quickly, but said nothing. Somehow she couldn't really tell if he ever told the truth. His face was hard to read.

"Maybe some day I can get more of the whys and

wherefores of your mother and how she coped, but I want to know how you were positioned in the family."

"Only son."

"Oh, I realize that – I mean other things specifically."

"I don't know –"

Then Bines stood up.

"What – did I say something?" Vera said.

"Never mind – never mind – we'll talk again – again sometime. I don't talk very much about my mom."

And he left.

He remembered Vera looking at him. The trees were pale when he went outside. It was growing dark. He drove back to town slowly, trying to remember what he had said.

Years ago Bines used to drive into town with his two dogs in the truck and a knife in his boot, and one day when the dogs started to fight he took his shotgun and shot one.

"Which one," someone had asked.

"The one on the left," Bines said.

When Constable Petrie came to his house to check the dog's feet with the plaster impression of a track he had received at the scene of a robbery, Bines said he had never had a dog with that big a track.

But he had shot one.

The one on the left.

"You didn't want to get bitten," someone had said.

"No, that's right – I didn't want to get bit," Bines said.

Then he bought another dog, and they all got along better.

At this time however he was not thinking of the dogs – he was thinking of Joe Walsh, and Rita, and the children, and his mother – years ago.

He went to see Alvin Savoie.

He sat there in the dark with half his face visible, and half in shadow. The moonlight played on the thin window and against the dusty room.

Alvin was married to Jerry's aunt, Frances, and Bines cared for her – and therefore for Alvin – as best he could. Alvin had lost his left arm because he had touched a wire, and was now on a pension of some sort. They had all kinds of kids about the house, and relatives of every description coming in and out.

"When Joe Walsh died I felt bad," Jerry said.

Alvin nodded and said that he had also.

"Good. If a woman comes to talk about me, say if Vera Pillar comes down here to see about me – about something – you say nothing about that tractor-trailer, Alvin – you say fuck-all about my father – you say fuck-all about my boy."

Alvin only looked at him, as if he hadn't heard.

"Say nothing about it – nothing about it – no – nothing about it."

Alvin said: "I never say anything anyway."

Jerry smiled. The air was turning cool in the house and the old dog hobbled up to Bines, so Bines reached down and flicked its ear with his fingers and smiled at it gently.

"Old Pepper – ole Pepper, fella," Bines said. The moon played in shadows on his back.

Lucy Savoie came from a family which had no power over anything. (The man from the camp made this observation to Andrew's mother while they were driving from the Texaco in Chatham Head. It was a bright day in June. The sun shone over the water and made it sparkle. The mill left a trail of smoke against the sky. Across the river, those small buildings where Lucy lived out her life seemed not at all dramatic.)

Lucy had worn the same dress to the first three grades at school. She remembered her mother being frightened of people and her father being obsequious, and her uncle Buddy, the man who Jerry Bines shot in 1986, coming in and terrorizing the whole family, saying he was going to burn them out or shoot their thumbs off, and all of the children would cry and tuck their thumbs under their fingers.

And then he would walk around amid all of them, turning about every now and then to glance at them, growling under his breath at them, and wiggling his own thumbs to show how well they worked. And talk about buying a pistol to kill the priest. It never seemed to matter what priest. Whenever anyone was going to make their first communion Buddy would talk about shooting the priest.

Amid all of this, amid the winter and summer, the squalid months of fights and botched silly plans, Lucy was the only one to stand up to him.

"I understand it now," the man said, coughing lightly because of the smoke from the mill as they went across the scrap-iron bridge in the heat. "I understand her courage now."

"Courage?" the mother said.

"Courage to stand against the inevitability of your own demise. Like in the way Jerry's father did at Kapyong – a battle so forgotten now in the annals of our miserable Canadian history books that well-heeled university boys will snigger at it in a second, and trivialize a grapple for life in the dark because they themselves have been ever protected from a slap in the head."

The house would smell of tea as strong as boiled beer, and everything in the house seemed to be brown. The light from the street came in from the window and turned brown. There was an old horsehair chair in the corner and a big black box sat in front of it.

They had indentured themselves so much to certain businessmen in town that her father Alvin could be telephoned in the middle of the night to nail campaign posters to poles, or to go to the bus station or train to meet someone and drive them home.

This happened on a regular basis.

Once, Lucy remembered, a man came into the house, a short man with the kind of ginger-coloured, finely tailored fur coat of a man who has always managed to make his life complete by acquiring things those around him did not have. And she remembered the worst terrible abuse coming from this man's mouth because her father had forgotten to move a crate for him.

This was the man, her father had told them, who had as much as a million dollars. He had also told them that he was in this man's will, and Lucy and her little sisters had always thought of this man, and how he was helping them, and how they would all be quite rich, just as soon as he died.

And then with all the children standing there he began to yell abuse at her father: "I don't need to take this from you, you rotten, no-good son of a bitch," he said to her father while their fish Timmy swam on its side in a bowl of milky water, wagging one fin. "You're a useless, no-good son of a bitch."

Alvin was sitting at the table, bent over, stirring his tea with a huge tablespoon. Every once in a while he would look up at the man and nod, and then put his head back down again.

Buddy always took control of the house when he came in, no matter how much they tried to get rid of him. In fact they often tried their best to bribe him to get him to go.

"You want that nice comforter, Buddy, darling – Buddy, dear?" Alvin would say.

"I have a few things to settle," Buddy would say.

"Buddy has a few things to settle, Frances – Buddy has," Alvin would say.

They would all be like mice waiting for him to come home from Dorchester Penitentiary. Each letter of his would be more ominous, more filled with foreboding:

"I'm on my way. Set up everything just right for me."

"I'm on my way. It won't be like last time. There will be no foolin with me this time. Love, Buddy."

Then he would come home. He would drink quite a bit, and then sleep. He would take little pills to stay awake, because he didn't want anyone fooling with him. He would stay awake because he didn't want to be tricked by them again.

He would walk about in his T-shirt, a bottle of flat lukewarm Alpine in his hand, shaking all over, sweating – all humble one moment and fierce and haughty the next, saying he was going to kill Jerry Bines.

Or he would say he was a mistake on life's part and wanted to die, and he would begin to draw lots, to see which of the children were going to have the privilege of dying with him.

Then he would sit on the stairs with only his toes visible to the little children sitting in the room below, and say that everyone had betrayed him, he had a list – he would flash this list out over the stairwell – and he would get them all back, sooner or later. And he had killed before (a lie) so it would be an easy matter for him to kill again (another lie). Like that, he would say, snapping his fingers.

He would talk about his mother and how she never got a good deal, and how he was going to burn people out, and how he had burned people out before.

The children would be sitting about the chairs in the living room or hugging against one another on the faded couch, which had an encyclopedia under it for a leg.

This would go on throughout the long winter day. He would talk and then there would be long periods of silence. Then when he spoke again they would realize he had moved his position a stair or two. Then he would come out and sit on the stairs with his guitar.

"Who knows this one?" he would say, strumming a chord. "'Talk back tremblin lips.'"

"'Shaky legs just don't stand there,'" some of the little children would chime in.

The sun would go down over the crusted red snowbanks. At twilight Buddy would come downstairs in his checkered coat and stand by the heavy winter door, with the rubber insulation torn up the side, looking out the windowpane at the road that hugged their house.

For years Lucy's mother Frances was frightened of him. For years she hid the children at night.

At times when Buddy came home he brought in people. People who came from Calgary and Edmonton or Nelson, B.C., and were wanted on Canada-wide warrants.

One in particular came in the summer of 1986. His name was Gary Percy Rils.

He was no taller than Lucy, but Buddy catered to him, and talked about them going to steal a tractor-trailer.

This was the first time Lucy remembered hearing of Jerry Bines (although she must have heard of him before). And when she first met him he seemed different from all the rest of them in the house. What people did or said never flustered him.

The man who owned the fur coat once came to the house to ask for him. "Tell him I'm busy," Jerry said, drinking a beer in the back room.

This impressed Lucy more than anything else. Besides this, he actually liked the children, called her Lucy-Woosie and bought her jawbreakers.

His hair was short, he wore an old black watch that his father had left him, studded like a dog collar.

Lucy knew, however, that there was some trouble with the tractor-trailer right from the start, and that this problem cooled the relationship between Jerry, on the one hand, and Buddy and Rils on the other.

At first there had been no problem. But once the problem came it seemed unsolvable.

It seemed Bines had made keys for Joe Walsh's tractor-trailer. He knew when it would be filled with cigarettes, how much time it would take to drive those back roads in the night, when to do it.

She'd heard that they drove to Pillar's Isle. Joe Walsh was Jerry's uncle and, because Jerry could not take the kind of calculated betrayal of him, he wanted to take the trailer back. They were to sell their cigarettes off to Vincent Paul, who was to sell them to a reserve in Quebec, but Jerry refused to allow it to happen.

Both Buddy and Rils thought Jerry was stealing the cigarettes from them. And things became more and more difficult at Alvin's house. Jerry simply said that no one was to touch the trailer until he said. And Gary Percy tried a different tack. He began to tease Jerry about being a hillbilly and about not being able to make up his mind.

"You'll find out when my mind is made up," Jerry said.

"Hillbilly," Gary Percy said.

"Ya," Buddy countered, as if he'd just thought about it. "Hillbilly."

One night Mr. Rils said he was going to cut Timmy open and have a fish fry. He picked the poor old goldfish – that had long ago dropped most of its gold – out of the bowl and watched it wiggle. Everyone was too frightened of the man to say anything.

But then Jerry, realizing it was the children's pet, told Rils to put it back. Rils looked at him for a moment in the sweltering night air.

"Put it back," Jerry said. "Won't be telling you no more – no more."

Rils put the fish back but Buddy began to say that it wasn't Jerry's house and he'd better not try that with him.

Often Jerry would bring them in a salmon or a piece of moose meat, some game or present for the children.

And of them all he liked Lucy the most. He liked her because of an incident that happened soon after he got to know her.

Bines had come into the house to visit and was drinking a quart of wine. He was looking out the window and a fight started across the road between two men. Jerry watched this for a moment without much interest, but then the little girl, Hazel, who was sitting on his knee, started to cry.

Jerry finished the wine, set the little girl down, and walked across the road. He hit one man over the head with the wine bottle, saying, "Stop makin noise." And he turned and walked back to the house.

By this time everyone in the house had scattered. The little girls – to Jerry, there always seemed to be a monstrous number of them – all ran to their back rooms and hid. Alvin also ran and when Jerry went back into the kitchen only Lucy was there. Jerry sucked at his bleeding right hand, and she ran to get something to wrap it.

In Alvin's home, during that summer that Buddy had brought Rils home, all the girls lay about in their bathing-suits but none of them ever seemed to get to the beach. The nearest beach was closed and long coats of slime came in with the tide. Frances walked about in her old housecoat, Buddy drank wine most of the day and shined his small car, and Alvin sat in the kitchen rubbing his hand across his balding head.

There was a hint of things going wrong with the tractor-trailer. At first everything had been fine, but Gary Percy Rils was impatient to take his money and go home – the fourteen thousand dollars that he said was coming to him. But Jerry seemed to be balking at this.

Jerry came in late at night and spoke to them, and sometimes Lucy would overhear the conversation.

The heat was oppressive in the house and half the little girls slept naked on the beds. Old trees cast their shadow gloomily through the window.

Jerry would sit on the couch in his jean jacket and pants, without a shirt, his sleeves rolled up halfway.

He would say that Joe Walsh had a heart condition and he didn't want him in any trouble.

He stared at them and they stared back. Buddy would sit on the ladder-backed chair in the hallway, with its back against the stairwell.

The old dog would hobble about between them, looking for Alvin, and then it would hobble out to its dish in the kitchen, near the sink, chomping on hard food, so that Buddy had nicknamed it Crunchface.

Lucy would come to the top of the stairs on her tip-toes and listen.

There was something about Buddy all summer. He kept tormenting Jerry.

"You're just scared of us," he would say in the dark so that Lucy could only make out his legs as they moved to tip the chair.

"Right," Bines would answer, or sometimes he wouldn't answer, the answer being made in a sort of cold silence.

"Scared of that big Indian Vincent too," Buddy would say. "I know who you're scared of –" Buddy would continue, "– scared of Gary Percy. Scared of Gary Percy," Buddy would say, as if it was a chant of a man on a rock in a storm. "Scared of that big Indian Vincent too –"

The days were long and silent and hot and Lucy would do her toes on the couch in the heat, while the baby, milk-white about the neck, slept with a heat rash on its cheeks, and the little girls, the heat making them blousy and sensuous, lay on the porch.

No one ever seemed to sleep. People walked about the house day and night, while the children cried on their beds and Frances sat in the corner with her head cocked and her ankles blue listening to the fights.

This is what Lucy remembered about that summer now. She never heard about the tractor-trailer after-wards except that, a week after the incident, Gary Percy Rils was caught trying to move it to Bathurst alone, and was sent to jail. And she did not know what happened to it.

After that summer, Jerry's wife never came back, and he lived alone with his grandmother.

3

It was June, ten months after Jerry Bines visited their camp. The man from the camp sat with Andrew and Andrew's mother outside under the patio awning in the small subsection of town that had been known at one time as Skunk Ridge but which had grown more prosperous and tenaciously middle class. The man had fine grey hair, almost blue in the light of the sun, and he continued with his story about Jerry Bines.

Andrew had not met Alvin or Lucy. He might have passed them a thousand times in the street, or walked by them in a store with his mother, or come upon them in a snowstorm as he walked home at night, and he would not know it.

But he knew the Pillars. He had met Vera when she came to the house to get his mother to sign a petition against the leghold trap. He had seen her at the recital at school. She belonged to Women for Women, the action group his mother belonged to, and a group for the ethical treatment of animals.

This was the woman who, people said, Jerry Bines had loved. And at the recital, while all the parents and children were standing in the hallway outside the auditorium, he wanted to get closer to her.

Vera must have thought it strange that this little boy was slowly edging up to her, slipping sideways through the crowd, and then finally standing right next to her and craning his neck to look up.

Her hair was thrust back and had spots of white in it. She had become locally famous, especially since she had published her book on Bines. The boy had wanted a copy of the book and they had gone down to the store but they couldn't find one.

"We sold it out, and there won't be any new ones in until next month."

"Oh," the boy said, disappointed. "I knew him, that's all," the boy said. "He was a friend of mine."

"A friend of yours?" the man said.

"Yes," Andrew said. "He was – a friend of mine."

Of course he romanticized Vera just as he had Bines. And he didn't think she would be older than his mother. But to him she looked like a lady. And the book wasn't called "Jerry Bines" as the boy thought it would be. It was called: *The Victims of Patriarchy (and Its Inevitable Social Results)*, and it was not a hard-bound book with a glossy picture on the cover like the *Hardy Boys*. The book itself looked like a thick scribbler – and it looked as if it had been just printed by a typewriter. There was, however, a picture of Jerry Bines on the inside cover. And the book was riddled with words like "sexual deviance," and "malfunction," and "dysfunctional," "hereditary masculine reaction," "empowering," "cross-addictive personality," and "impacting" – all of which the boy stumbled over and became bored with. The worst of it was, to the boy, the book had no life. It did not show how Jerry Bines shook your hand.

"The book was just to get back at her ex-husband, Nevin, for the emotional violence thing," the man said. "That's all. Anyway, I think the relationship between Jerry and Ralphie is more important in the end, to be the only friend Jerry had at the last."

Ralphie was to meet him twice in a row.

Both meetings were peculiar to say the least.

4

Ralphie believed he had seen the last of him. During the middle of October he was working on behalf of the Kinsmen, collecting money for the Hospital for Sick Children in Halifax.

One evening Jerry Bines was waiting for him when he came out of his shop. It was raining and cold. There was a slight fog in the earth. Jerry seemed nervous, or impatient. "You know where I live?" he said.

"Yes, I think so," Ralphie answered.

"Well, I have something for you – so come up to supper – up to supper tomorrow night."

Jerry then mentioned something about his truck and never alluded to the supper again. But, for some reason, after Ralphie said that he could make it, Jerry looked very pleased with himself.

He went to Jerry's house the next night without telling Adele where he was going.

Jerry's grandmother lived upstairs, and Jerry lived alone downstairs. He opened the curtains when he saw Ralphie and waved.

He had to put his two dogs away and then went to let Ralphie in.

Bines sat down and focused his attention on Ralphie, and smiled slightly at him. The house was very nice – the downstairs was furnished in oak and pine; the chesterfield was at an angle to the bay window so you could watch the hummingbird feeder and the stream.

"Workin today," he said.

Ralphie, for some reason, felt the discomfort of being under scrutiny. But Jerry Bines did not understand this.

Jerry looked sideways and cocked his head as he spoke. His eyes never looked at Ralphie for long. When he caught a reaction to his look he would look away, to the side, with his arms folded, and speak out of the side of his mouth.

"Like salmon?" Bines asked.

"Yes," Ralphie said, smiling.

"Good. Gram is cooking salmon."

There was a silence. Ralphie could actually count ten seconds going by.

"I have something for you," Bines said finally. "In the back. What are you worried about – the dogs?"

"No," Ralphie said.

"Dogs won't touch you," Bines said gently. And he smiled as if to reassure him.

They got up and moved into the back room. It was huge and cold. The carcass of a buck deer was hanging, though deer season didn't start for another two days. It seemed to startle Ralphie, the buck with its front legs stiff, the cool room.

"Here you go," Bines said. "For your little boys and girls."

In the corner were three wheelchairs.

"I always liked children," Jerry said. "I have a little boy."

He watched the expression on Ralphie's face.

"Little crippled boys and girls – it's a shame," Bines said, watching him quietly. "It's good doing things for people," he added quickly. "I always like to, anyways." There was just a touch of hesitation in his last remark because he had been waiting for Ralphie to say something. And Ralphie knew this.

But Ralphie did not know what to say or do. He looked at Bines and nodded, and started to speak but didn't. He just looked at the chairs again, and the whole moment, instead of being a happy one, became a painful one.

Bines then started to show Ralphie how they worked.

"Foot-rest flips down right here," he said. "Look –

there's a motor on this one —" He smiled as he sat in the motorized wheelchair. "Ha ha," he said, "look at me."

Jerry laughed. Then he glanced at him, and got out of the wheelchair as if he had belittled his original intention. It was obvious that for a moment neither of them knew what to say – and then he motioned for Ralphie to go back inside. "Well, never mind them for now," he said.

When Ralphie left the room he could feel Bines' eyes on the back of his neck.

"They're great, Jerry," he said, turning around, and he almost fell when he turned. Jerry grabbed him, so quickly Ralphie didn't even see the hand come out, and held him steady.

"Well, never mind about them for now," Jerry said.

Bines never mentioned the chairs again. Ralphie then tried to talk about them enthusiastically, but Bines said nothing.

When Ralphie woke the next morning he forgot how he had gotten home. He stumbled from bed to look and see if the car was in the yard.

Then he sat down in the chair in the corner of the room and tried to think. Daylight was breaking over the trees. The old school he had gone to as a child looked harsh and silent across the street.

He had talked too much – it was Bines' eyes resting upon him that made him. He had told Bines about himself – about the feasibility study he had done on an oil pipeline a few years ago. About its complete failure – and his complete failure.

He had worked day and night for months on end, only to have all he did trivialized. And his data not used. It was a government-subsidized study, and they used data from a firm in the States that did not have the province's interests at stake.

Ralphie told him about this and the waste of a quarter of a million dollars, just to see if our own oil could be pumped to us. And they decided that it couldn't – and that it was for the good of us if it was not. They had tried to get both the British and the Americans interested in Hibernia again.

"I'd get even with them," Jerry said matter-of-factly.

"No, no," Ralphie said, shrugging in a way which suggested that he actually could get even if he wanted to, and that he knew what getting even meant.

But the strange thing Ralphie noticed was that Bines did not know where our oil came from. Then, of course, the feasibility study struck Bines as ludicrous. If we had oil in our own country, why buy it from somewhere else?

For a moment he thought that Ralphie was joking with him, and it became very painful.

"Who are these British and Americans to run and bull us?" Jerry said.

"But it's all true," Ralphie said, mentioning the name of the man he had worked for.

"Haaa," Bines said abruptly, as if, if Ralphie laughed, then he would know he was fooling. "Haaa – oil pipeline," he said. "Oil pipeline – pipeline," he repeated, looking down and rubbing his pants. Then he glanced away cautiously.

"If I hear anything about it I'll let you know," he added, because he always said that to people who admired him for being a powerful man. That is, he must have thought that Ralphie wanted his help in some way.

"I'll let ya know," he said again, nodding to no one in particular. But his eyes looked puzzled for a moment and he ran his thick callused hands through his hair, as if, for some purely instinctive reason, he felt he had to look more himself.

§

Vera's ex-husband, Nevin White, looked like a little old man though he was only forty-five.

"Everyone tormented him, not always through design," the man told Andrew. "It was in a way heroic that he stayed here – stayed in a room by the bridge.

"The reason he stayed in his unbearable room was for the sake of his daughter. Even when the custody battle was over. For two years he did not see the girl or speak to her. He was not allowed. But for those two years he watched her from a video he had made of her sixth birthday party. After those two years he was

57

allowed one Saturday a month on condition of Vera's approval. At times Vera gave this approval, and at times she didn't. And then, seeing a mark on Hadley's bottom one afternoon, she accused him of incest. It was never proven.

"I knew Nevin at university," the man continued. "I used to play a lot of bridge then. I never liked him, but now I would say there was something brave about him.

"He tried to take his own life in 1987. But it didn't work. These things never do if you wake again in the morning.

"Pills are a rather womanish way to go in the face of so much violence on this river," the man maintained. "And so people began to tease him and call him Aspirin-head.

"And yet it didn't seem that way – that is, womanish (if we can use that term anymore); it didn't seem that way. It only seemed that he was a broken man. And it might have been a defiant and even heroic act. Heroics have their own way of adapting.

"He moved from rooming house to rooming house, with his pictures of Hadley and his video. And then one afternoon in October of 1989 he was suddenly filled with new confidence and hope. Vera telephoned him, wanting to see him. And she sounded very pleasant. It took him a day to get up the courage to see her. To bathe and shave and iron his pants and shirt."

The boy asked when in October this was, and the man said that it was the day of Jerry's first visit to Vera's house. Jerry had missed meeting Nevin that day by twenty minutes.

"When Nevin got to the house he found out that Vera wanted only one thing, however – she wanted to change Hadley's name to hers. Coldness always has its roots in sensible thought.

"Then she asked him if he would remove his hat. As yet she hadn't looked at him. She was working on a computer, and staring at the screen, with earphones on.

"He took his hat off, sat down, and put it on his knee. He had never seen her working on a computer before, and he was bemused by this. He was bemused because he felt, like Jerry was to feel later on, that he had been left behind forever. He caught a glimpse of himself in the mirror. He had practised what he would say to her for an entire day, in just such a mirror, and now he hated his reflection. His hair was thin and drawn back into a ponytail, turning grey. It was as if he suddenly realized he had not moved in twenty years, while the world had spun away.

"When she finally glanced at him, he felt his lips begin to tremble and he looked away.

"He said 'No!' He wanted to leave Hadley's name as it was. And then he said, in a confused state, that she had no right to ask him this. As soon as he said this he felt that she had turned against him forever – and that no matter what he did nothing could 'turn back the page' for him and Hadley. That he would go into the dark without either hand to hold. Vera's hands were long and mannish and yet he remembered only how gentle they could be.

"He held his hat clumsily in his hand and looked down at his cracked and blistered boots.

"'You are being unreasonable,' Vera said calmly, continuing to type away, looking at her computer screen – the final draft of an article on aboriginal hunting rights, and the land-track claims certain reserves here had.

"When he looked up Hadley was there on the stairs, listening. As always he wanted to see if she was wearing anything that he had bought her. He smiled, yet when he went to speak to her, she ran upstairs.

"Don't be misinformed about it. Nevin didn't pity himself. He hated himself. Worst of all he hated his own posturing, his lack of manliness, is what it came to. He remembered running away one night, from bullies, and leaving his first wife, Gail, alone on the street. While he hid. Back in 1970. All of us at the university knew about this. At the time people made a series of explanations for it, saying he was nonviolent, et cetera; but this only made us queasy later on. I don't know how else to explain it.

"But don't be fooled. In a way he was filled with integrity and so could never forget it. He had tried to make up for this act all of his life. And, in a way, it was this act which had caused him to leave his first wife and blame her for things she did not do. And finally take refuge in Vera's domination of him – with the calculated pretence that this, in itself, was manly.

"Perhaps he was a man struggling to be brave in a world he did not understand. Once you run you almost always run forever.

"So even here he had to suffer the robust torment from teenaged boys. You take that when you are not perceived to be brave. What he had run away from in 1970, he was still haunted by today.

"But" the man said, "they had done an odious thing – they – those street kids who hung about the building – had broken into his small room and had stolen his VCR and, along with it, his video of Hadley. He knew who it was, but they didn't give it back. And he, like so many people, was unwilling to go to the police. This was his own Golgotha, his Calvary – unknown, of course, to himself.

"The boys stealing his video set in him, within a matter of days, a strange insistence that it was all the fault of Jerry Bines. No one really understood why.

"And late at night, wearing his torn coat, a pair of dark heavy-rimmed glasses that were taped in the middle, and tan cowboy boots, he would make his way back to his room, lie on his cot smoking, and fall asleep with the television on."

How did Bines and Nevin meet? They met through the inevitable wanderings, the man said. They were bound to meet because they missed each other by seconds so often. Nevin had moved his room six times in the last three years, always within the space of a mile or less, very near to where Jerry stayed when he was in town.

They met at Alvin's on October 17 – this was in the final police report. It had been pale all day and, by night, a few sharp tiny flakes of snow began to fall, near the school, and down over the great grounds.

Throughout the day of October 17, Nevin slept. He tried to sleep most of the day. It was almost dark when he got up.

In fact, the lights were on down the street, above the tavern. There was a little light off by a side shed.

He went downstairs to check his mail. He was waiting for a letter from his father, because he had written to him to ask for three thousand dollars. Then, moving across the street, he turned towards the Savoies'.

As Nevin went out Bines was in a building down the street.

Bines had heard that Gary Percy had escaped from jail and he wanted to know if it was true. He had come to ask a friend.

"I heard the same thing," his friend said.

In the back room there were hundreds of videos, movies of all descriptions.

The walls were heavy and paint-chipped. At the far end of the roof there was a hole, and you could hear pigeons thick in the autumn air, and a feather or two stuck against the tin siding's rivets. This was once a video-games room but was now being cleared out. It was a building that would become something else. Jerry tried to think of what it would become and then forgot about it.

The man who owned it, Abrey Smith, was the only man Jerry admired and wished he had become – to control money and assets and small-town politics – but he had not become this.

This was something, as Loretta Bines told Constable Petrie three months later, that Bines was either lesser than or greater than – but could never be.

"Maybe they'll catch him before he gets here," the man said, about Gary Percy.

"Jail, ya – good fuckin place for him," Jerry said.

Jerry went out into the dark, ten minutes after Nevin. He turned in the same direction, along the same battered street.

So this is how they met, the man said: Lucy wore one of Jerry's old jean jackets. She had a Sunoco hat on her head. Her winter boots were wrinkled like an accordion on her legs, and her breasts were small, and pointed sharply against her light sweater.

Nevin was at the house, rolling a cigarette out of his Drum tobacco, and being very officious about doing this. Finishing rolling his smoke, he lit it and sat back with his feet crossed on the table. The wind blew outside, and it was dark. Bines came in and shut the door behind him and, noticing Nevin, said nothing. It was perhaps the first time they had met face to face, although no one could be sure. Nevin had been on the jury that had acquitted Bines.

Jerry asked Alvin something – and then looked in the fridge for a beer.

"No beer, Frannie," Jerry said. "No beer here?"

"No beer," Frances said.

Jerry seemed annoyed by this and everyone was silent.

"I can get some beer," Nevin said, startled by his own voice.

"Get us some beer, then," Alvin said.

Nevin stood up.

"Sure, I can get some beer – I can get some. I'll have to walk," he said. "It might take a while. Lucy, will you come with me?"

Lucy said no, but Jerry looked at her and nodded his head.

"Oh, I suppose," she said.

And they left the house.

They went down the dark street, the man continued. The autumn night was bitter. The streets were bare, except for a slick of black ice here and there.

Lucy coughed into her hand and buttoned her jacket up, and glanced sideways at him, her arms folded across her jean jacket as they moved.

They went to his apartment and he furtively opened the tin box, where he kept his money. Some people thought he had a lot of money. Then he went to the liquor store and bought a case of beer and some wine, and they went back to the house.

Jerry was sitting in the same place, with a parka and sleeping bag at his feet. Nevin had seen this parka and sleeping bag in Alvin's closet before. But, the man maintained, Alvin had always mysteriously refused to allow Nevin to wear the parka, though he wanted to desperately. And now the mystery that had surrounded them was gone. They were Jerry's.

The wine Nevin bought had a cork, but no one had a corkscrew.

A breeze blew against the window, and smoke from chimneys trailed away or was snapped in two, scattering beneath the stars.

Jerry wore a parka himself, with a toque on his head, and an old knitted beige sweater. The one thing everyone noticed was how proportionately strong his body looked.

"I'll run back to my apartment and get my corkscrew," Nevin said.

Nevin walked by him, and Jerry moved his foot slightly to let him pass. For some reason Nevin thought that this was some form of reprimand. He thought of the young boys who had stolen his video of Hadley and resolved never to mention them to anyone.

He ran home once again. Out of breath, he took all his utensils out and looked at them over and over and over – three forks, four spoons, four knives.

Finally he went back to the house, dejected.

The wine bottle was opened on the table, and half-empty. Jerry had opened it with his buck-knife.

Nevin went back and sat down in the corner. Now and again he would smooth his hair with his yellowish fingers, and sniff because his nose was running. He took a beer and sipped on it.

Although he didn't speak initially, after a while he began to say things, and the more he drank the less he was able to control what he said.

The next morning he felt that he had said something terrible, though he couldn't be sure. Like always, he went about his room searching for cigarette butts.

Then, as always, a vague picture began to take shape. A hand, a noise in the corner, Lucy saying no, a person looking at him as he spoke, and he began to realize something.

It was the parka and sleeping bag. He kept asking Jerry if he could have the parka, since Jerry had his video of Hadley. And Bines had tried to ignore him. But when he went to reach for the parka under the chair, Bines had reached his hand over and squeezed his wrist. That was all – the hand coming out to stop him from picking up the parka. And yet it seemed to Nevin emblematic of everything that was going to happen.

Later that day Nevin, still drinking, went back to see Lucy and Alvin. His hair was tied in a ponytail at the back, and he wore a pair of gumboots over his pants. The air was clear and raw and had stayed that way all day. Although the TV was on, and all the children were crowded about watching, Nevin took no interest in this. He was bothered by a problem.

The problem was not thought out, yet it was heavy upon him. Why did he feel more guilty about the sins he had done in his life than Jerry felt about what he had done. Why was this? Who was happier? Who was more at ease?

He sat for a while not speaking, and not able to look at anyone. In fact, all he did was stare at a part of the old chair, where, he remembered, Jerry had sat the night before. Then suddenly he decided to tell Frances and Lucy what he knew about Jerry, thinking that they themselves wouldn't know.

"He has a bad reputation," he said. "He has a little boy who has leukemia and he doesn't provide for him. He robbed more than one family here."

"Who says?" Lucy asked. Her eyes were fixed upon him and there was a curious, cold smile on her face. The breakfast dishes were still sitting on the table and Frances was sitting beside them, her head cocked in a peculiar way, as if she did not know whether to laugh or not.

"Oh, it's what I heard," he said. "So it's best if we stay away from him."

Frances coughed and looked scared at this remark.

"Well," Nevin said, as if he did not want to upset

anyone. "I'm certain he stole my video of Hadley – still, no one wants you to be mean to him. It's how he was brought up." And then he turned to Frances and said: "It's bad for your mother to have him around too, Lucy."

"Jerry's dad was Frannie's brother," Lucy said quietly.

"Oh," Nevin said. He looked over at Frances who had her head cocked slightly. And he blushed. Then he felt cold.

"Jerry's dad was wounded in Korea," Lucy said. "In fact, he was disabled because of that – and Jerry took care of him the best he could."

"Oh," Nevin said. "Is that the way it goes?" He remembered now that the man Jerry had shot in 1986 was Buddy Savoie.

And suddenly he looked about the little brown room. There were tea stains all over the wall where Alvin had thrown his cups when he got mad at the children – especially on Sundays. There was a long picture on one wall of a regiment of soldiers, and another of a man in an air-force uniform standing in the park.

"Oh," Nevin said. "Well, still – that doesn't excuse Jerry, does it?"

"Nothing excuses anyone," Lucy said. "When my dad touched a wire and lost his arm Jerry was the one to climb the tower at Millbank and get him down."

"Yes," Nevin said, upset with himself, "well, we all climb towers, don't we –"

The old dog, with its back matted with fur, and one

68

ear chewed off, and its face carrying a perpetual look of dishonour, hobbled down the stairs and clicked across the tiled floor wagging its tail miserably. This, and the pictures of the soldiers, made Nevin feel uncomfortable, as if he should get up and leave.

A man can be born anywhere and go anywhere. But to live your life in a place far from where you are born, it's best to be in a city. A man ending up in a small town, as Nevin had, is readily adrift.

He stood to go, his ponytail hanging flat against his neck.

As far as Bines was concerned he had nothing to do with Nevin. He did not know or care about him.

"Vera's ex-husband or something," he would say. "Ya, I've seen him. He was on the jury that let me go."

He did not particularly like him and he did not like his ponytail, but he didn't care what he did. The principal things that Nevin remembered were with Bines all passed over. (The hand reaching out to stop him from taking a parka, opening his wine with a buck-knife.) But then there was the idea of the video. Nevin had been telling people that Bines had his video of Hadley.

Bines was angry at this but he had gone into town to find out about it. Within a half-hour he had the video in his possession.

Then he told Lucy to go over to the apartment and take Nevin his video back.

"Give him his video back – it's all he had of that little girl."

"Oh dammit," Lucy said, "why didn't he get it back for himself?"

Bines knew Lucy did not like Nevin – but he was Vera's ex-husband and Vera had been nice to him, so he wanted to take no sides. Besides, the boys had tormented Nevin about the video long enough – and it was time to give it back.

"I don't know what's wrong with Constable Petrie," he told Alvin suddenly. "I say hello, how are you, and the next day he's up at my house with a dog looking for cocaine and a shotgun pointed at my head, with Gram trying to hit him with a broom. That's no good."

He took the video out of his pocket and placed it on the table, then drummed his fingers softly.

"You take that down to Nevin," he said to Lucy, nodding at his own generosity.

Always with Bines, one action should prove everything. He was giving the video back not for Nevin but for Vera. When Vera found this out she would like him – and therefore, he conjectured, write a better story about him. He did not consciously think this – until later on – but he felt pleased when he placed the video down.

"He's been after me for years," he said.

"Who?" Alvin said.

"Petrie – I done nothin to him."

"I know, I know," Alvin said, but he smiled slightly.

It was the smile of someone who is happy that misfortune has happened to someone else. In fact, Jerry had suspected Alvin of informing Petrie on him more than once.

"Lucy," Jerry said, just as Lucy was going out the door. Lucy turned to him. Her hat was pulled down over her eyes, her hair was tossed up under it. She had three studs in each ear. "Tell Nevin not to bother me no more," he said simply. "No more." And this immediately erased Alvin's annoying smile.

Jerry went out to his truck, as the first snow fell against the flat grey windows on the street. A week passed before anyone saw him again.

5

By June the air was still and great fields of hay lay hot in the sun near the stream that smelled of small fish and flat rocks and the bittersweet longing scent of shale gravel under the bridge.

Andrew did not know how close he was to the centre of the conflagration until his mother's boyfriend – that is, the man who had taken him to the camp last September – told him.

"Oh, he lived right over there," the man said.

"He did?"

"Right across the river in that white house."

There was nothing about the house one way or the other that looked unusual or spectacular. There were some flat boards out back lying in the small triangle between the shed and the back door. There was a back porch, where Bines supposedly unwrapped his eyes at 3:00 on the morning he came from the hospital.

"And that's where Rils came in to shoot him," the boy said excitedly.

"No – that wasn't here – that was at his wife's house."

The heat made the air soundless and sweet and the branches were filled with new leaves. The boy's mother had just bought him a fishing rod, so the man could take him out fishing, and he felt sorry for them both – felt sympathy for his mother for buying him this rod and sorry too for the man.

Andrew's uncle had come with them today. And the two men began to discuss Bines.

The boy looked over at the house. Its back window was closed. Some shrubs sat in the warm air, and under the blue sky they could see a bird-feeder on a stick.

"How long was Mr. Rils in town?" the boy asked, try-ing to bait a hook, and sound grown up, and watching as the worm dangled into the water and then was swept into the eddies a few feet away.

"Oh, a week or two."

"Last December."

"And Vera found out and became angry with Bines."

"No, Vera never knew much about what was going on," the uncle maintained.

The whole idea the two men spoke about was that Bines had somehow reached toward another world,

Vera's world, and had for a moment tried to divorce himself from the world he was in. Now one of the men countered that that too was a falsehood. And Vera knew this.

And they went over point by point what Jerry gave and what he would want for it. If he gave kindness he would want devotion.

The boy had not seen Bines much at all.

Last fall Bines had come into the camp again to help them retrieve a moose. There was sleet in the air and the trees were dark. The men had searched for the moose all afternoon and then one of them had gone to get Jerry to help. He arrived at about 10:00 that night.

"Who shot it?" Bines had said.

"I did," the boy's uncle said.

"How many?"

"How many what?"

"How many times did you hit it?"

"Only once."

"What were you using?"

"A .308."

"Well, that would bring it down – bring it down," Jerry said. "Anyway," he said, "we'll go find the calf – because the calf won't leave it."

The men hadn't thought about the calf, and when they got into the trucks for the long ride back to the chopdown everyone was silent.

Jerry took a light from his truck and went into the

woods and walked for about fifteen minutes about the perimeter.

"It's over here," he said, and then he told the boy's uncle to bring him the gun.

Now, as the boy thought back to that night, and how it had stormed later on, he thought about how the talk centred on Jerry's wife, Loretta Bines.

"He brought her down a long way," someone said, as the boy lay in his bunk. "What a kind, sweet little girl she was –"

"His first wife – no one hears of her anymore – he took them both down."

And again the boy felt uneasy lying there in his bunk safe and warm, and he felt that Jerry Bines was outside of life.

When he asked about this now the man told him that no one was outside of life.

"Some people just have more of a chance than others, and some just have to take the chances that they have. I know a lot of people who were more unfortunate than Jerry Bines, who turned out much better –"

The day was warm and filled with new life, and it was only June, which meant he had the whole summer to go.

6

When Bines went to Vera's house he often stared at the
little girl with her curly hair as if he was questioning
something. He would smile at Hadley, take a quarter out
of his pocket, and flip it along the back of his hand, con-
trolling it magically along the top of his knuckles. Then
he would pretend to hide it behind his head and find it
in her ear.

This act of the quarter along his knuckle brought
laughter into the house.

What he was questioning he wasn't sure about. But it
had something to do with Hadley's empty world. This is
what he came to think of as he did these tricks for her,
and made her and Vera laugh. It didn't matter usually

what type of world other people had. But he thought Vera was a very unhappy person, and that this showed in the little girl's sudden tantrums, and most of all in the drawings she brought from school. It was a world that had nothing because Vera was too conscientious to be a consumer. What people took for granted in their homes, Vera herself agonized over buying. So there was no cable TV, no VCR, and in the end no happiness either. And all of this was considered diligent, and practical.

In the kind of world Vera had constructed – the kind of statistical world – there were concepts Bines thought were false.

He had no notion why these things bothered him, but the air was cool and winter was coming, and Vera's questions were now more and more personal.

She asked questions that should not be asked. And he did not know why he had agreed to all of this. (He had agreed perhaps because he thought he would become famous.)

"How often did your father beat you? Can this be attributable to your fear of men – I mean did it engender a sense of powerlessness? And did you beat your boy?"

He did not know how to answer this and smiled.

"I assume you know your problem is you fear men – this is the constant in male violence."

But Bines said nothing. He shrugged and looked at her a second, so that she looked away quickly.

"I'm sorry," she said.

And she actually did seem to be sorry. He smiled.

"It don't matter – don't matter," he said. He scratched his ear. "Don't know – don't know – the old lad hit me when he was drunk –"

All of these questions bothered him, and yet still he cared for her.

"Nevin hits children. I know he hit Hadley once." She whispered this.

"I don't want to know," he said. And he stood up. "Don't want to know."

"Oh," she said.

He felt strangely disheartened that she would say this about his son – as if nothing he said seemed to get through to her, and he resolved to introduce his son to them at the earliest opportunity.

"That'll straighten things out," he thought as he left the house.

By now he knew very well that she was using him. He did not know why. But he was too smart not to know. Perhaps to get back at Nevin – perhaps to prove to her friends how wild she was – or how bored she was – perhaps to become famous herself.

Whatever it was she was using him.

He moved the quarter along his hand, and flipped it with his thumb, unseen, into the air.

The man told this story:

Jerry had never known truth, but he had conceived it

78

himself like some great men conceive of truth and chisel it into the world. And it was his and no one else's.

He was like some great soul cast out and trying to find shelter in the storm.

His mother used to sing to him. He had never admitted he was afraid. He remembered those songs when he was a little boy and went to church wearing the suit his mother had bought him, and his father was at the picnic. His father had a plate in his head and would want to fight. And the Matheson boys would always try to get him home.

His father would stand with his shirt out weaving back and forth, his right fist cocked a little, back against the wall, and the dry earth, the smell of hay, tumbling with the crickets and smell of summer and all the world jostling in trumpets of song – a mentally unfit melancholy man along a road with a little boy by the hand.

Then you know truth.

You don't know it before then. (This is what he could not tell Vera, of course.) You don't know it before then.

And the Matheson boys go home, you see, thinking his father would be all right, now that the picnic is over and the thumb wedge of darkness is over the trees, and it is going to rain.

Down by the brook with tall delicate sweet grass along the borders, the flies flick out at the last of an August evening.

A cow bellows somewhere off aways. I love you all I love you all.

And the small sifting sand of passing cars blown up as the man walks home in his squalid suit jacket, with a small boy by the hand.

But the men he was going to fight, who had all tormented him, are there on the road. The men, one of whom was married three days before and is on his honeymoon, a man named Gary Percy Rils, is drinking wine with the boys behind the barn near where your father was pitching horseshoes in the dust.

At first it is not an argument and you are still sitting there watching your dad, who at one time was a fine fellow – a long time ago. But then it is arguing. It is always arguing and arguing. And you watch carefully – the man who is just married is wanting to fight – you know him from before.

And your father is frightened. You see that. And the Matheson boys intervene. No one pretends he is frightened. None pretend he is. But he is all alone, and has his little boy.

And your father smiles at you as if it is a joke and everyone is friends and whips his mouth with his hand and takes a bolt of dark whisky.

You don't know when they are there exactly – it is August and you are going home with your father and it is starting to rain.

I love you all I love you all.

And then the car plays with you on the road.

And you want to help.

Your father picks up a rock and you stand behind

him and his leg is shaking. And you never forget how he tries to protect you, this hobbled, mentally unbalanced, melancholy man.

"Grrr," he says, with the rock in his hand, and the headlights flicking on and off, the grill mashed with flies, the wilted carnation from the wedding sitting on the dash.

"I have my little boy," your father pleads. "I have my little boy – Jerry – is just a little boy."

In the dark, by the ditch, with the crooked brook, going home.

I love you all I love you all.

7

Ralphie now felt himself lucky – a privileged part of the town. At first he did not admit that he felt this. But after a while it became evident that he did feel this way, and that he could no longer hide this feeling from himself.

It was good to know Jerry Bines because Jerry Bines was either liked or feared. And it was evident that people now looked upon Ralphie this way also. That is, that if Jerry Bines liked him then no one would bother him.

It was strange, because all of his life Ralphie had reacted with aversion to this kind of manipulation. But now, within the sanctuary of it, it all seemed different. It seemed possible that the things Jerry did were misconstrued, were even wonderful – (the story about him escaping from prison one time now seemed a wonderful story). And Ralphie also knew that within the government, within academic circles, the same kind of manipulation happened. But complementing this was another bothersome feeling that perhaps no one, not even Adele, knew. At first it wasn't noticeable but lately it had become prevalent.

Last week Constable Petrie had come to tell him and Vera that Gary Percy Rils had escaped from prison. Ralphie had not thought of him in years, even though Gary had made death threats personally toward him.

And Ralphie's feeling now was – in the most secret part of his being – that he did not want this man in his life and hoped Jerry would help him – even if Jerry had to go to prison or die. It would make him and Vera safe from someone who had plagued their family for twenty-odd years. He tried not to let on he felt this, just as a man tries to let on he does not feel pleasure at an accident on the road.

But how could he ask for help? He worried about this constantly. Of course Constable Petrie told him that Gary Percy Rils would never get here to bother him. But still and all there was this edge on things, and Ralphie would think, "If only my father had not been the judge who heard the case."

The case was in 1960. Gary Percy Rils had beat up a

young man and left him for dead. The man had three small children. He was an average man who had opened up a small store in Millerton. A good, kind-hearted man. The fight had started over cigarettes.

After he was beaten up he suffered from a punctured kidney, a damaged hand, and was blind in one eye. He was tormented by painful fluid and was frightened, and yelled at the children if they made noise.

He refused to stay in the store unless his wife was there, and could no longer play the pipe organ in the church. Gary Percy was given three years in prison.

"So it is me who is going to suffer," Ralphie thought after Petrie told him about Rils, and he disliked himself for thinking this, yet he also suddenly disliked the idea that the man had played the pipe organ.

"Everyone must suffer – one for the other," came the answer.

And this idea that everyone must suffer one for the other – which had been extracted from Ralphie's thoughts on calculus more than from his study of St. Paul – made no difference once you yourself began to suffer. Once you yourself began to suffer you wanted the suffering to stop, and you would allow someone else to take it and bear it for you. (That this was the parable of Christ made no serious imprint on Ralphie, who disliked religion.)

He wanted to ask Jerry for help in this matter. But how do you do this? Straightforwardly or stumbling? And what were you doing if you did ask for help?

Ralphie had a map in his office upstairs. Besides doing tests on water samples taken from the river for his independent study on effluents from the mill, and a more serious study on groundwater that he was engaged in, he was also engaged in a kind of detective work.

He was plotting Gary Percy Rils' imaginary course back home, from various police reports, and wondering if he would ever make his way, and then the feeling came over him that he was quite willing to have someone else suffer instead of himself.

To Jerry it would be nothing. And he had heard rumours that Jerry didn't like Rils anyway. (Ralphie in his innocence never bothered to wonder why this might be.) But this feeling, this other feeling that he would be willing to have someone else suffer instead of himself, plagued him.

One night he got up late and went into his office. The naked tree branches were tapping the window. He was standing in bare feet and long underwear looking at the map. There was a tiny bit of snow on the ground and everyone was sleeping. He believed Rils to be some-where in Quebec – it was only an intuition, a feeling.

"No, I can't ask Jerry – I'm his friend," Ralphie thought. "I'm his friend."

And at that moment a feeling of peace descended upon him.

The peace lingered a long time in the cool night air. And yet he shivered as he went back to bed.

He only knew that if something terrible happened to

his life, it would be because he had been born. In this he was only the same as everyone else, like the poor man who played the organ at the church.

On November 3, Ralphie promised Bines he'd go to see him.

All day he was worried about it. He didn't know why Jerry would want him to go, though he pretended to himself that this was not worrying him.

There was a fresh load of wood piled at the back of Bines' house, and when he got out of the car there was the smell of the silt of deep fall in the air. The river gurgled down below and turned away at the wide bend towards dark heavy trees.

He went to the door but suddenly felt a hand on his shoulder.

"'Lo," Bines said. He was wearing his toque and his army parka, with its attached fur hood sitting down on his shoulders. The toque made his head look small. His eyes seemed mildly annoyed. "Come on way in," he said.

And he swung the door open to let Ralphie pass.

"Got someone for ya to meet – ta meet here," he said. "Come here," he said.

Ralphie looked at the kitchen door that was only half open – it didn't open any wider – and a young boy of about three or four squeezed through it.

His hair was blond and his face was pale. He had a

small mole on his neck. He was clutching a small wheel in his hand.

"This is William – William – this is Mr. Pillar – he's a friend of mine."

And William came over with his hand out to shake Ralphie's hand. It was as if, and Ralphie was certain of this, Jerry had rehearsed this with him all day.

"Excuse me, Mr. Pillar," the boy said, and then looked at his father worried and flushed.

Jerry smiled. "What do you mean, excuse me?"

"I mean – hello, Mr. Pillar." And he put his hand out again.

Jerry smiled again.

Ralphie took the small warm hand in his.

"My young lad," Jerry said.

They were putting the boy's wagon together and Jerry had been out to the shed to get some tools.

He went back into the kitchen and sat over the wagon, with William standing beside him holding the wheel. Two dogs sat in the corner with their heads on their paws.

Now and then Jerry would ask William to hand him something, or to take something from him and put it away.

"Put this in the box," he would say, or, "Hand me that axle."

And silently, and with great interest, the boy watched as his wagon was assembled. Now and then he looked up at Ralphie and smiled.

"Mr. Pillar's been to university," Jerry said, with an inflection of absolute respect, so that his son would also show it.

When the wagon was finished, Jerry told William to get ready for bed and that he would make toast for a lunch.

"Got your pyjamas?" Jerry said. "Didn't your mom send no slippers down?"

The boy sat at the table, with his eyes resting on Ralphie. His face was delicate, and his small ears stuck out just slightly. He looked very pale, and somehow not entirely of this world.

After the boy went to bed Jerry came back downstairs.

"His mother's a Pentecostal girl – from upriver," Jerry said. He laughed slightly. Then became serious. "That's all right though – that's all right."

In the light, and warmth of the stove, Ralphie noticed Bines' hands. He was always noticing things about him, as if trying to decipher something.

"You know," Bines said, enthusiastically, as if Ralphie would like this, "I coulda shot a moose yesterday – I didn't – didn't shoot it – no – I said, that's that, Ralphie Pillar."

He smiled again. It was as if he was admitting to a weakness. And Ralphie looked down at his rubber overshoes for a second. Again he felt he had done something wrong in looking away when Bines was speaking of something that was suddenly important to him, but he could not help it. And Bines' reaction was to look at him questioningly a moment, and then to look away also. Then Bines cleared his throat and tried to think of something else to say. He spoke quietly. "I like children," he said, after a moment. "Poor little kids – some never have nothin –" he paused as if reflecting on something, as if he realized he had said this before. There was another terrible silence, pregnant in the still house.

What he wanted to ask Ralphie about was the continents. How many continents were there? Where was Russia? Why was Russia like it was? How many war planes did Russia have?

And then he asked if there were people from other planets.

"I don't know," Ralphie said, smiling slightly.

"Well, how many other planets is there?" Bines said.

"Billions," Ralphie said.

Bines said nothing. Every now and again there was a static sound from the other room.

"What's that?" Ralphie asked.

"Police scanner," Jerry said. "I have to know what's going on here – my young lad is asking me about the continents and I said, I'll see about it." Then he grinned, and said: "I don't know very much – very much –"

"Sure you do," Ralphie said, the way he would lie easily and comfortably with other people.

Bines answered this by getting up and opening two beer.

But then he felt embarrassed.

"When you were in school – I was in Kingsclear. Never learned nothing. My young lad'll know all of that anyhow – sooner or later – I don't care about it – but it'll be good for him – for him anyways," he said.

Bines had told his son this story. It was just before Willie went to bed. Bines was sitting, facing his son, with his huge hands folded near Willie's knees. Every now and then Bines would touch those knees with his hands, and draw them away delicately.

It was a story about a deer and how it outsmarted a hunter. It was a story of the woods, of gloom and darkness, of autumn ending and winter coming on.

"This happened a long time ago," Bines said. "There was an old deer, who had been in many battles in many ruts, and this was its ninth year. It had been cold all autumn, and the trees were naked and raw. Far off it could see smoke from the hunter's house, rising in the sky. It had lost its strength – this old buck – and kept only one doe, who had a small fawn. The afternoons were half-dark and winter was coming on hard – and the hunter kept coming – the hunters always keep coming."

Bines looked over at Ralphie and smiled, and Ralphie nodded.

"The big deer didn't have no friends. He usually travelled alone. But he saw all the other deer being killed, one by one. And though he gave them other bucks advice – gave them advice – they didn't follow it.

"So all the other deer was killed, one by one. But the hunter who tracked him – who tracked the old buck in the snow – was smart as any hunter. The buck knew this, and wanted to keep him away from the doe and her fawn if he could. He was an old deer and the doe was young. So the big buck decided to draw the hunter to himself – and each day the food was more and more scarce, and each day it was colder. And each day it led the hunter farther and farther from the cabin.

"The puddles were frozen and the trees were naked, and the sky moved all day long –"

Jerry touched the boy's knees lightly again and smiled.

"Every day the hunter would get closer – get closer to the doe. But the buck had a plan, which it had learned from living so long. It would always show itself to the hunter at daylight and lead him on a chase throughout the whole day. The hunter could never catch up to it. At the end of every day when the hunter came to the river the buck wouldn't be there. The buck always disappeared – and its tracks disappeared, as if it had flowed away."

"Where?" the boy asked.

"The hunter didn't know – didn't know. No one did. The hunter too was tired. He was a tired man. Each day he got up earlier. And remember – each day he wanted deer meat for his family. So he was only doing what he had to. Had to do there. Each day he concentrated on the buck – each day he followed the tracks to the river. Each day he found nothing there.

"And each day his children were hungry, his wife was sick. And each day the hunter was weaker and colder. And each day the big old buck had allowed the little doe and its fawn to live another hour, another night."

Jerry looked about the room, and the boy smiled timidly.

"The buck was old and tired but so was the hunter. The hunter had a bad hand and had wrapped it in his leg stockings. His eyes were fine and could pick out a small bird in a thick bush. He scanned the river every evening. The river was a wild river and had just made ice – a wild river there, but the ice was thin.

"One day after a heavy snowfall the hunter found himself deep in the woods – the sky had cleared, the stars was coming out – the hunter had been following the buck for many hours. It was hours I guess he had followed the buck that day.

"There wasn't a sound when the hunter come to the river.

"The day was solid and still and he cursed to think he had lost it again. Lost that buck there again. Now the stumps were covered and everything was quiet. Afternoon was almost ended – and night was coming on – and that's when he saw the doe. She was making her way along the riverbank, and he could just make out her brown hide by a tree. She was coming right toward him. It was almost dark. She hadn't seen him, and she was leading her fawn toward him up an old deer trail. The fawn behind her.

"So the hunter felt he must use this chance, and he knelt and aimed and waited. Everything was still. He cocked his old rifle and was about to fire – about to shoot it, you know. But then of course everyone knows what happened."

Bines paused and lit a cigarette. He smiled and touched the boy lightly on the knee once more.

"What happened?" Ralphie asked.

Bines drew on the cigarette and looked about.

"Everyone knows what happened," Bines said. "It has been passed down from generation to generation to all the smart deer in the woods."

"What happened?" Willie asked.

"The hunter aimed his rifle, and suddenly the ground moved – the ground under him – and the buck come up, from its hiding place under the snow, right under the hunter's feet – under his feet – everyone knows that – and snorting and roaring ran onto the river. The doe turned and jumped away, and led her fawn to safety.

"And the hunter made a mistake, mistake there – hunters always do sooner or later – I mean make a mistake there. He was so angry he didn't think straight.

"'I got you now,' he yelled, and he ran onto the river too.

"Now, that river could hold the buck, and it could hold the hunter. But it could not hold both together. And the buck turned and stood, waiting for him to come further out. The old buck never moved. And if he was scared he never showed it.

"And when the hunter got close the buck smiled – and the ice broke, and both of them went together – down together into the wild rapids – clinging to each other as they were swept away. And this story was passed down. It's a passed-down story.

"Now the end is going to come – in one fashion or another," Bines said, softly, and again he turned to Ralphie and smiled. "We all know, the end will come. You either face your hunters or run from them."

After the boy was asleep Bines began to ask Ralphie questions. He asked about Ralphie's assets – the shop. He wanted to know how much the computers Ralphie sold cost. He knew Ralphie's family had been wealthy, and it was a wealth Bines could not fathom.

"You mean yer dad just bought that sailboat, like that?"

"Yes," Ralphie admitted. "Just before he died, he bought a huge sailboat and left it downriver. He never used it. And it rotted. Mom never wanted it, nor would she let me sell it or use it. After much indecision, she gave it to Vera. But Vera couldn't stand to look at it – Vera thinks all of these things are a part of privilege and doesn't want them. Besides Vera didn't like Dad. I may as well tell you that."

Bines reflected on this a moment.

"My old man was a cook on the tug for a while," he said, nodding. "And I got to go on a ride one day – one day." He smiled. He then thought of something else.

He said that he liked Vera, that she was the smartest person he had ever met. "So if she didn't want to use that sailboat – she must be right," he said.

"She's very bright," Ralphie agreed.

Bines then said, "I don't like Nevin though – he's said things against me."

There was an uncomfortable pause.

"You wouldn't bother Nevin?" Ralphie said.

Bines stared at Ralphie a moment, quizzically.

"I'll never bother Nevin – I promise," he said. "Nevin has a lot of money too, does he?"

"I don't think he has very much of anything, any more," Ralphie said. "He once had about fifty thousand. But I think all of that is gone."

Bines was quiet for a moment. Then he smiled. He said he wanted to know why Ralphie played bridge, why was it considered such a good game, and who played it with him. When Ralphie told him why he thought it was the one great card game and the names of some of the people who played with him, Bines said, "I bet you could teach me to play, Ralphie – I could learn. Loretta'd be some surprised at that – me playing bridge."

He looked at Ralphie, as if Ralphie should be as surprised and happy at this new idea as he seemed to be. Ralphie smiled, but he know the smile gave him away.

"So," Bines said, his tone just slightly less enthusiastic, "when could you teach me?"

"Oh, I don't know," Ralphie said. "I play on Saturday nights. I'm pretty busy with things – I have new computers coming into the shop – I mean soon. But I could teach you."

"Sure," Bines said, without flinching, "I could come down to see you on Thursday night – and learn to play bridge – and meet yer other friends. I never learned much – I hear it's a good pastime. A good pastime, anyway."

And then he nodded to no one at all.

In the middle of the night Jerry left the house, and his son. He moved along the road in his truck, and felt the late dark cold upon his skin. The river was silent, ice and gravel in the ditches.

At 2:00 he was at the house of his friend, Vincent Paul.

Vincent was still up, sitting in the living room, and one of the women was in the kitchen. There was a young man on the floor in the corner.

When Jerry came in Vincent looked at his wife. Vincent had a huge beer gut, his hands were huge, and he wore a bracelet on his left wrist.

Vincent spoke Micmac to the young man in the corner, who looked about suddenly.

Then the woman said something in a merry, humorous voice.

For years Vincent and he had been friends, selling moose meat and deer and thousands of pounds of salmon taken from Indian nets the government couldn't control. Jerry did not care that Vincent slaughtered out of season in the name of moral retribution.

Jerry sat down on the arm of the couch with the door half-opened behind him. The moon played down on the half-finished house that as yet had no front steps. The light in the kitchen was warm, and some of it splashed on Jerry's pants. When he spoke the young man stopped laughing. "Have you heard from him?" he said.

"No, no," Vincent said, absorbed as he was in his television program. Jerry hardly ever watched television and had never understood the fascination for it. Just as he had never understood the absorption or the fascination over hockey or baseball.

Vincent was wearing an Indian emblem about his head, in the new-found politicism that had emerged over the last few months because of aboriginal concerns in Ottawa. And this too seemed to justify a morally hurt expression on his face. But Jerry knew all the ways there were to deceive yourself in order to trample on a friend.

He took out a pint of rum and shook it, holding it lightly in his hand, first at Vincent, then at the boy, and then at the woman. The woman took a drink. Jerry smiled. Vincent yawned. There is no moralizing like the moralizing of the damned. And Jerry knew this quite well.

When he got up to go Vincent looked sideways at him and cleared his throat.

"See you, dere, Jerry – ya, see you," he said when Jerry left. Out in the dark he heard the boy speak and Vincent's soft chuckle.

Jerry smiled as he had learned to do whenever he felt danger or was in pain.

There was nothing that was not calculated in Jerry Bines. He was drawn to Ralphie now – because Ralphie exhibited traits that he wished he himself had. But in the strangest way he was also naive – he thought Ralphie would not like him. So he had to try to learn how to speak about "important" things, though every time he tried to talk about these things he saw Ralphie become embarrassed, and he didn't know what to do.

If anything bothered him, this did. Why did Ralphie look away when he mentioned he didn't shoot the moose – or when he got him the wheelchairs for the children? He felt, in both instances, he must have done something wrong. He had had to go to Rogersville to get the chairs and spent half the day in the police station because they wondered why he was there. Perhaps this is what Ralphie found out.

"I like children," he'd told Ralphie. "I always have."

Not only was this true, but he'd thought that this was the ingredient which would clear everything up. But Ralphie, for some reason, didn't seem to believe him.

He didn't know why, so he had invited Ralphie up to meet the boy – but again the same look of being surprised and out of place had come over him.

He had tried to glean some information about the feasibility study too – about the job consultant position Ralphie had, and late one afternoon last month he went to Moncton and waited on a side street, staring at the lights in an old stone building.

Then at about seven in the evening a man came out and walked by him. Jerry took a breath, shrugged, and got out of the truck. He grabbed him by the collar and hustled him behind the wall.

"Don't be stealing people's ideas – that's worse than killin someone," Bines had said as they moved.

The man had no idea what he was talking about. He tried to move but Jerry held him firm.

"You ruined his life," Bines said. "You stole his ideas and ruined all his work – it all went for nothing – that's no good at all."

"Who, who?" the man said.

But Bines could not say "who," he could only leave it at that. And so he did.

By morning it was snowing softly. It had covered the stumps at the edge of his property and Jerry was looking out the window and contemplating something. His little boy sat at the table eating his cereal.

Bines was in his pants and T-shirt, which showed him to be far stronger than he looked with his shirt on. There was a frown on his face as he watched the snow coming down and being drawn away in white circular wisps by the wind.

"Yer mother still go to that church?" he asked.

"Yes," William said. William was shy of him also, and he knew this. Though he had never touched the boy or laid a hand on him the boy had heard so many stories about him that Bines would sometimes see his boy shaking slightly when he walked up to him.

And it didn't matter if he made him the wagon or got him the sprocket for the bicycle, or, sometimes, though only on occasion, patted his head.

"I got ya some Freezies on a deal – I got a deal on Freezies – you want a Freezie?" Bines said.

The boy looked at him a second. Freezies were for the summer, but Bines didn't consider this.

The boy nodded.

"Ya, I got a Freezie for ya," Bines said, going to the

fridge and taking one out of the freezer. He bit it open with his teeth and passed it to his son.

"There ya go – Freezie for ya," he smiled. "Freezie for ya."

Then he sat down at the table cautiously, and drummed his fingers up and down.

"Do you know how many planets there are – there are billions of planets," he said. "I read that in a book – you tell yer mom."

8

The reason Bines was liked was this: in most ways in his life he had willed himself to be, and made people conform to his will – not so much by physical strength as by a brutal nature, and was surprised when they did not conform, was, in fact, puzzled if they did not. And this was something that Adele had seen and that those who had come up against him, even when he was fifteen and at Kingsclear, had seen.

A few days later he went to Vera to talk about his son.

He looked at her and smiled slightly. He asked her if she would help him get Willie to the hospital in Halifax as soon as possible – any delay was dangerous for the boy.

"I can see about it," Vera said.

"See about it – that's good – see about it," he said.

"Life hasn't treated you very well, has it?" Vera said, and suddenly she smiled, staring at his callused hands and a scar above his eyes, the tattoo of a star on the skin between his thumb and forefinger.

"No, no – not so bad," he said.

"Well, you've had a much harder life than most," Vera said.

The day was rigidly cold, the sky blue, the trees with naked branches soared above the town. The streets were bare and yet cold filthy snow clung to their edges. It was November and the colours of Christmas decorations were starting to appear about the street.

"No, no," Bines said, "my own fault – own fault there – where's Ralphie – huntin?"

She stared at him quietly. "No, he doesn't hunt," she said.

"No, don't hunt no more very much meself – very much – see those little deer – seems a shame to shoot them."

And Vera smiled slightly.

"Anyone to do that to a woman should be shot," he said, lifting his right hand just slightly to the poster behind her head showing a woman and a child cowering while a man was about to strike them.

It doesn't stop, the poster read, it just gets worse.

"Oh yes," she said, turning to look quickly behind her. "Yes," she said.

"Woman can't defend herself – herself as much," he said, contemplating the picture again. "Old man – my old man was a rough old cocksucker," he said.

Vera was surprised he had said that word but he was so unassuming when he said it that she smiled slightly.

"Mister man," he said but his eyes were far away, as if he was thinking of something and didn't realize she was there.

By their meeting he found out that she had contacted the hospital but there was nothing she could do.

"Everything that can be done is being done – Mr. Bines refuses to realize this," she was told.

When she explained this to him, Bines simply nodded.

"I'm sorry," she said.

But he didn't answer. And then he spoke of other things.

What he wanted to know about was Nevin. And when he found out that Vera was keeping Hadley away from him he was disturbed.

"Well, maybe you should let him see the little girl – little girl there," Bines said to her. "Straighten him around, he's all upset about something."

"Nevin has to come to grips with himself," Vera said. "I can't help him anymore."

"No, no," Bines said, "I see."

"His father was a bully patriarch who terrified him, like mine was to me, and he has to come to grips with it."

"What's that?" Jerry said.

"A man who dominates others," Vera said.

"Oh ya – that's no good," Bines said. "No good."

He looked away from her. And suddenly she said: "I'm afraid of what will happen to Hadley. It's what almost happened to me."

"What did?" Bines asked.

"Incest."

Bines was quiet then. He looked at her a moment and said nothing, but things went over in his brain like tumblers in a safe. Incest – he wasn't quite sure what it was. He scratched his jaw and looked about. "You stick with me," he said, "and no one'll ever ever bother you again."

But he didn't know what else to say.

"Hadley doesn't like her father anyway – she's frightened of men," she said, then paused a moment. "I'm not saying your little boy is frightened of you."

"Don't know," Bines said. "Hope not – hope not." He cleared his throat and moved his hand through his hair.

She had a small display of books along one wall of her office and he looked at them. The titles to him were so obscure and grandiose. He was thinking of buying his son a book. He looked at the titles wondering if he could catch a glimpse of a title his son would like, and when she caught him doing it he lowered his eyes.

105

For all the times they met Bines kept his answers short and to some point he wanted to make. He would, in fact, answer either yes or no to most things.

Vera would sit opposite him, staring at him as he spoke. But slowly he felt he had given away too much information about certain things, and not enough about others, and this bothered him.

One night he gave her information the impact of which she probably did not fully grasp. He spoke about the tractor-trailer filled with cigarettes that had been stolen in 1986. He spoke about Joe Walsh being investigated because he was its driver and did not report it stolen for forty-eight hours. He spoke of Joe's heart condition, and his losing his job.

"The man who set it up had to turn around – turn around and save Joe – couldn't let him take the blame."

"I see," she said, but she was far more interested in Jerry Bines and did not know who this man was.

"What about 1977?" she said. "What started the trouble that year – your father died? In what way do you think of it, looking back."

Bines had quit school in grade five. This was the first thing Vera learned that proved her stereotype. And he had turned pro at eighteen and had four fights – his weight varied from middle to above light heavy, and he fought light heavies to heavies. But he wasn't disciplined and at least twice he entered the ring half-drunk. The only thing he had on him that was really above average was a left hook like a Philadelphia club fighter, but he was always off balance when he threw it so the other fighter could move to his right and counter Bines on the top of the head. So he quit the ring. And, the man said, he was responsible for a number of things which he did not tell Vera about and a number of things which he did.

But surely Adele knew. And this is why, concerned for Ralphie, she finally drove up to see Bines.

The man wasn't sure when this was. It could have been as late as the third week of December.

There was the house that she hadn't visited since she was a little girl, and a house in some ways which she had always feared and in it a person she had always feared also.

A dog snarled in the cold night. If it had been the third week in December the shotgun hole in the wall would have been made — so it had to be that late. Because Adele asked him about it.

Bines was sitting in his sock feet by the stove, and he had the scanner on, listening to the police broadcasts.

"Oh, that," he said, about the shotgun hole. "Well, I gotta fix that. I'm trying to quit this smoking racket – I have this gum – it don't do a thing for me – just makes my teeth numb." And he smiled at her. "I also got a beeper – cost me a hundred dollars. You're only spose to smoke during the beeps – I never figured it out."

And he took it out of his pocket and showed it to her.

"That's what I should get," she said.

"Here," he said, handing it to her immediately.

"I can't take it," she said.

"Go on – it's yours – yours," he said. "Quit smokin – it's yours."

Then he got up to get her tea.

"I don't need any tea," she said shyly.

"Well, you don't drink – so I'll make you some tea," he said. And he went into the kitchen.

Always one act for Bines proved his ultimately generous nature, which in the common man would never be seen as anything more than civil.

Bines was struggling at this time. Of course at this time he was almost blind in his left eye but no one knew it.

This was close to the end, so there was a lot going on that Adele did not know.

But he desperately wanted to make a good impression on her – because of Vera who he had fallen in love with as one falls in love with his teacher, as university sophomores idolize their professors.

Of course, Bines did not know quite how to make a good impression on anyone. He had qualities greater and lesser than the qualities it took to make oneself socially acceptable.

He had been beaten all his life, and beat back. He had enemies everywhere, and like most of the wounded he had always kept himself physically fit to ward off those who might come against him.

"I don't want Ralphie to get into trouble, Jerry," she

said haltingly, "so I'm coming to you as a favour – for Joe and Rita, if they were alive."

"Trouble – Ralphie wouldn't get into any trouble," he said, and then with the same unfathomable sense of self he had, a sense of self that always in some important way disregards others, he moved his hand through his coarse hair and smiled at her.

When he went into the kitchen she noticed that his grandmother was lying on the couch, on her back.

"Is your gram sick?" she said.

The wind howled; there was snow against the window, and an old potted plant sat in the corner.

"I don't know – check her pulse. She's been drunk as a loon the last three days. Most likely still with us," he said. And then he went into the corner and brought out a steel ball and joint.

"This is what they took out of her hip – and replaced it with a plastic one – lift that."

"It's heavy," Adele said.

"She's been dragging that about with her for five years – and look at this." Here he lifted the old lady up.

"Don't wake her," Adele said.

"See that – she's got a brace from her bum to her neck – if she doesn't wear it she bends in two – it's a sorry racket –"

When they went out into the night air, the stars had spread their canopy over the heavens above the crowded trees and furiously frozen wastes.

Jerry put his arm around her, the first time he had

done this since they were children, and pulled her toward him.

"Come here – I want to show you my pet."

And he took her to the pen by the shed.

It was the dog that had snarled at her. But it was not a dog, it was a coyote.

"I was drivin on my Ski-doo and came across it eating on a fawn, so I run it over and brought it home – and it gets up and starts to walk away – so I grabbed it by the tail and threw it in here. I don't know what to do with it."

"Why don't you let it go?"

"Let it go," he said.

Adele nodded, her scarf wrapped about her face, so that only her eyes could be seen.

Bines opened the pen, and the coyote slouched on its belly as all coyotes do and then dashed towards the field.

"There ya go, Delly," he said. "There ya go."

And Adele could not help but feel what so many others felt when they met him, that she was in the presence of an extraordinary man. For what reason she would never really discover.

9

Nevin had wanted to change his visiting date, but Vera said that wouldn't be possible. Nor was Hadley any longer allowed to visit his apartment.

So, finally he went to visit her. All the way there he was trying to think of what to say to her. "I know you're a good person – a kind person – and everything like that – but I can't change her name."

He walked to her house. It was after 7:00 at night. The river stretched out beneath him and the wind snapped the trees. The grey night seemed heavy, and scuds of snow unravelled on the frozen earth.

Nevin had come up from the street below, which was almost bare and smelled of supper. His feet were cold, and his eyes stung. Suddenly he stopped, not knowing what to do.

Jerry Bines' truck was in the yard.

It was as if he was seeing a crude joke at his expense. In fact he did not at first realize it was Bines' truck. Snow began to fall down from the sky over the heavy branches. A cat scurried and stopped to notice him, wind blowing its fur so it seemed as if it had a hole in its back.

Hadley wasn't allowed pets of any kind because of her allergies. She wasn't allowed anything. She went to school and came home, and Nevin remembered that the only time she ever tattled at school seemed worse simply because of her nature.

And thinking of this as he saw the cat, he walked across the street, and went into the house.

Bines was sitting in a chair with his arms crossed and two huge rings on his fingers – rings that could slash Nevin's face in a second.

"What are you doing here?" Nevin said. He took a cigarette out of his pocket and held it in his hand. Bines looked over at Vera and then looked away – as if something had distracted him and Nevin was not important.

Vera said nothing. But at this moment Hadley became her major concern and she ran to get her – as if something horrible might happen. And at this moment Nevin smiled weakly, because he was unsure why she did that. Later he realized that this was the worst part – but that it also was orchestrated. That by doing this she had cast a calculated moral judgement – and part of her enjoyed it.

Bines glanced at him. "Be here if I want." He said this very calmly – as utterly calm as a man could possibly say it.

"You have your own wife and son. Why don't you go there?" Nevin said.

Bines said nothing.

"I'm not frightened of you," Nevin said.

"No one asking you to be frightened of me," Bines said.

"Then what are you doing here?

Bines looked at Vera. Nevin remembered that at this point Vera shook her head for some reason, and was hugging Hadley.

Again Nevin remembered that he said something he felt was horrible but he couldn't stop himself. "What in hell did you ever learn? You can't even read very well – that's what Ralphie told me. He laughs about it at his shop – all the time."

"No one's asking you to be frightened a me," Bines said again. He was hurt by the remark about Ralphie and didn't know how else to answer.

"Can't even read," Nevin said. "So Vera feels sorry for you – just like she feels sorry for Lucy – and all those people."

"No one told you to be frightened of me," Bines said.

"Well, I'm not," Nevin said. "And you got a sick little boy – what are you doing here? You should be home with him. At least I don't have a sick little boy."

Bines again looked at him, more puzzled than before.

"My boy'll do all right," Bines said. He turned away from him, like you would turn away from someone who is sick, and then he stood and went into the kitchen to get a glass of water.

Nevin was still talking away in the other room. And then he started to complain. He was saying that all he wanted to do was to visit with Hadley and no one would let him. That all he wanted to do was hug his child.

When Bines came back Nevin was sitting there as if everything had been drained out of him. He went to reach out for Bines' hand and shake it. And then he began to follow him about the room with his hand out. "Here we go, brother – here we go. Little mixup. Here we go."

Bines, who had not paid attention to him while he was doing this, turned to him while he was putting his parka on. "Go sit down," he said calmly. "Sit down."

And Nevin did actually go and sit down. "Hadley," Nevin spoke. "Hadley, you understand."

And as Bines was leaving Nevin said: "Jerry – I'm sorry about your son."

Damp snowflakes fell out of the sky, and birds flitted in the crevices of half-empty doorways below Nevin's room. There was a smell of cold harsh salt and bread.

Why did he leave his first wife? It was at university. Of course, he didn't give a damn for divorce or marriage. But there was something else. She had waited for him at home all one night in January of 1971. It was his birthday. And the next morning when he came in, the cake was covered and left on the table in the kitchen.

"I've met someone – Vera Pillar – so you should know," he said. And he couldn't help feeling vindictive. "She is a woman with her own mind about things – not like you."

He remembered her smiling at him timidly, as if he were joking, and then she lowered her eyes and sat on the bed clutching her left thumb with her right hand.

"So I thought you should know," he said to her angrily, blaming her for things she had not done.

Now he remembered another incident painfully. It was Hallowe'en and Vera and he were living with a group of friends on University Avenue.

Instead of giving a group of little boys and girls treats they brought them into the house and scared them. Of course, this was a long time ago, and Nevin was only young. But what was supposed to be a joke turned mean.

And what he most remembered about that night was a little boy trying bravely to protect his sister when she started to cry.

Twenty years had passed and he had not forgotten a moment of that terrible encounter.

Can you imagine growing up like Jerry? he thought suddenly. He'd heard of Jerry's father, who'd had a plate in his head, and had beat him unconscious "whenever there was a full moon," Nevin had heard.

But, of course, there really was no way to help him. And every time he saw him, it always seemed to startle him, and he looked away in fear.

And he knew that Jerry disliked him.

And his little boy was sick. Which was awful. Especially now coming on to Christmas. How could a man as powerful as Jerry have a child who was sick?

This is what bothered Nevin. Secretly he had, in a way – as most men in town – admired Jerry Bines. And yet when he saw his powerful body striding up to the house he realized what he should have realized years ago – that nothing Jerry did or said, or how he acted, could make any difference, in ways which were real.

For twenty years Nevin had remembered the little boy hugging his sister. For twenty years he remembered his first wife holding her thumb and smiling, first timidly and then peevishly, at the corner of the room. And both these recollections could assault him in a second more powerfully than any Jerry Bines or Vera Pillar. Because he had not been kind, when some law greater than his required him to be.

It happened at the schoolhouse Hadley went to. All the children had been warned about Nevin numerous times. It was like a great treat for them to see him, and to tell the teacher.

"There he is," they would say, "over by the pole."

And the teacher would go to the window and look out. Nevin would be looking across the street towards them. Then he would turn and walk back down the hill.

This had gone on most of the fall. All the children were now conscious of who he was and why he was there and, though they were told not to speak to him, sometimes they would yell at him at recess.

"Na na, na na na – na na, na na na," they would chant. And then they would all run over near the empty swing and look back at him.

"Don't say na na, na na na," Nevin would say.

"Come and get us," the children would yell. "Na na, na na, na na. Come and get us."

"I don't want to come and get you," Nevin would answer. "Who told you that?

"Ah, go 'way," the children would yell. "Na na, na na na."

One day when he walked up the street to stand near the pole he suddenly saw a man come out of the bushes on one side and a woman walk across the lawn towards him. Both exits had been cut off, and he was not allowed to go on to the school property. He walked out into the middle of the street.

"What are you doing here?" the man asked. He was

younger than Nevin – much younger – and the principal of the school.

Nevin reached in his pocket to haul out his ID and show it to him. He smiled at the man as if he could clear all of this up.

"I don't want to see your ID," the man said.

"We have one hundred twenty children to look after," the woman said to him. "If you come back here again we'll call the police – make no mistake."

Nevin was wearing huge mittens and an old hat with kamikaze-style earflaps. His hair waved in the wind under it, and his checked woods jacket was opened, with a vest underneath.

"I can come here if I want – I want to see my daughter."

"Ms. Pillar has made it quite clear that you are not allowed to see your daughter."

"But she's a goofball," Nevin said, because he did not know what else to say. "She's made everything up."

The woman looked up at him with such clear hatred, such a testimony of dislike, that he felt she had been informed about him in some vast and terrible way.

"I've given up everything," Nevin said, in a voice that seemed to come from some faraway part of himself – and he remembered as a little boy at school being punched in the stomach by an older boy. He had not thought of this in forty years. But now it seemed to come so vividly clear to him – the boy's fist and the smile on his face when Nevin fell down, and the dark stone of the old brown school, and the wet pebbles he fell on.

"I'm coming to get her tomorrow and we are going to Woodstock." He did not know why he said this, and he did not know whether he meant Woodstock, New Brunswick, or Woodstock, New York.

"Fine," the principal said. "You've been warned."

Nevin did not go back the next day. Nor the day after. But three days later he returned and stood at the pole. He had a suitcase in his hand. He had nothing inside of it, but he thought he should bring along a suitcase. He stood there for about ten minutes and looked towards the white building and then up towards the train station.

Suddenly, in back of him, a police car pulled over. Nevin went to step out of the way, and he was thinking: "They are coming too close to that pole." He made a gesture as if to wave the car on when he saw another police car turn off the town hill and come towards him. He began to back away but suddenly one car drove right up to him, and the other car pulled over.

In two seconds Nevin was wrestled to the ground, turned over on his back, and handcuffs placed on him. All the while he made a great effort to explain things and kept trying to clutch the suitcase in his hand.

The next day Nevin carried a knife when he went to the tavern. Everyone knew he was carrying this knife.

Because Nevin said he was going to kill himself as soon as he had a beer. "Maybe two beer – and then I'll do it."

He wore his old boots and his coat. The sky was bright blue that afternoon but a few stars could be seen by 2:00. The air smelled of wood smoke.

Jerry had heard all about the knife. And Nevin having it on him.

Jerry came into the tavern at 4:00. He looked at Nevin, saw his old coat and hat and turned-up salted boots, and looked away.

He went to the back so that, because of the wall, Nevin could not see him, and ordered a beer.

But five minutes later, rising from his seat twice, then hesitating, Nevin came over to his table.

Jerry looked at the knife sticking out of Nevin's pocket and picked up his beer slowly and drank, just a sip, and put the glass down.

But suddenly Nevin trembled, and had the strange desire to confess things. He wanted to tell Jerry about his past, about what he had done at university – that Hallowe'en night when the little boy came to the door and he had tormented him. So Bines would understand him better. And he began talking to him. "Vera has given a sworn statement."

"Oh – about what?" Jerry said.

"About Hadley being terrified of me," Nevin said, "and about my attempted suicide."

Bines didn't speak. He shrugged and looked out the

window. There were too many other things on his mind at the moment.

"I've never touched Hadley, but Vera is so certain of it – I don't know, she almost has me convinced. It all comes from her past. I go there and Hadley hides behind a chair – she is only a little girl. I say to her: 'Hadley, do you want your name to be a nice name like White, or a silly name like Pillar?' And she shouts out 'Pillar' and runs down the hall. All the children call her Pillar, and everything –"

"Well – that's too bad – too bad," Jerry said. He didn't know what else to say.

"I come from Massachusetts," Nevin said. "I was at Woodstock – a lot of people only talk about Woodstock but I was actually there."

But Jerry knew nothing about this. Or why it would be important. He shrugged. Some snow lay on the barrel outside and birds pecked at crusts of bread while water dripped in the middle of the afternoon.

Nevin told the story about all the trials he had had with his father, who had bullied him and had made him stay in on Friday night and made him get his hair cut and wouldn't give him the car for the prom, and Jerry listened. Finally his dad and he had a fight over Vietnam and he came to Canada – where he first enrolled in Business Administration at the University of New Brunswick. But then he met this tall young woman. He told Jerry how he had tormented his first wife – and belittled her.

"I got mixed up in the Strax affair," Nevin said, "Vera and I."

"I don't know what that is," Bines said.

"It was a movement in the sixties at the university," Nevin said, and, screwing up his eyes and trying to think, he continued: "It was positive – it was a positive thing."

He told Jerry he went on protest marches, and burned the American flag – well, he did all the things the American children did.

But Bines had not heard of this. And it did not matter to him at all what people did. He simply shrugged. His face had a tanned look, his eyes were bolt-black and each pupil seemed to shine in more than one place.

Suddenly Nevin said: "Dr. Leach has me on a bunch of pills."

And he took out these pills – his blue ones and his yellow ones and laid the bottles on the table.

Nevin paused and lit a cigarette and looked around the room. A fierce wind blew across the street over the blue ice, which at twilight had turned deep violet. The shades of night were in the store windows.

Then he smiled uncertainly and looked down at his blue pills and his yellow ones, the butt end of a knife sticking out of his coat pocket.

Bines got up and left the table and he did it so abruptly that Nevin thought he was going to hit him. And he closed his eyes as if waiting to be punched.

But Bines went out of the tavern to his truck and

came back before Nevin had his pills put away. "Read this here," he said, and he left a book on the table. "It might help ya. It's what Joe Walsh gave me when I was in jail – I don't know, I never read it – never read it – but a lad in jail like you read it – as far as I know about it – and he is working over at Canadian Tire and doing okay – okay as far as I can tell –"

It was called *Sobriety Without End*.

Nevin looked at it. Bines had placed it down near the bottle of yellow pills.

When he looked up Bines had gone.

10

It was about 6:00 at night on November 19 when Lucy came to the door. She hardly glanced at Ralphie Pillar, just now and then looked up under an old cap as she spoke. "Jerry wants to see you," she said.

"Jerry Bines – where is he?" Ralphie said.

"He's in the hospital – so you have to come."

The house was five or six blocks from the hospital. The trees were naked and a hard wind blew against their faces.

"What happened?" Ralphie asked.

"I don't know," Lucy said. Her jacket was short and thin and her arms were folded. Her boots scraped the pavement in time to the hurried motion of her hips.

Ralphie had not seen him in a while. Bines had never phoned him, had only once been to the house. Bines was not a friend of his in the ordinary sense.

When he and Lucy got to the hospital, he did not know what to expect or how to enter the room. That is, in the most basic way he did not know whether to look sad or smile, and he suddenly realized he had the same feeling when he had gone to visit his father years ago.

Bines was not in bed. That was the first thing that Ralphie had not expected. He was sitting in a wheelchair, side on, with the window slightly open – the window opened from the top – trying to get some air. The sky and earth were frozen solid now.

The nurse was trying to get Bines to go back to bed. Bines was listening to her, without speaking himself. Then Ralphie noticed, when Bines tilted his head, that his eyes were wrapped.

"You have to get back into bed, Jerry," the nurse was saying.

"No, no – going home."

"Oh dear – you can't go home tonight."

But Bines paid no attention to her.

"God, Ralphie," she said, "what are we going to do with him?"

And she said this as if everyone knew Bines and was at a loss as to how to handle him because he was so wild, and that somehow this was wonderful.

But Bines paid no attention to her.

"What happened to you?" Ralphie said. He looked at

the wrapping and he went to touch Bines on the shoulder but didn't.

"Camp blew up," Bines said.

"What?"

"Camp – blew me right through the door – the door," Bines said.

"How are you?" Ralphie said.

"None too pleased about it," Bines said.

Everyone was amazed that he had lived. Not only lived but that he'd only suffered a broken rib and a flash to his eyes.

"It's a miracle he's alive at all," the nurse said.

Bines said nothing. He didn't even seem to notice what people said about him, or that people were gushing over him or that people were amazed by him.

He told Ralphie that there was nothing left of the camp, except the door.

Bines kept touching the wrapping about his eyes, almost in slow motion, with the tip of his fingers, and turning his head slightly when Lucy spoke, or Ralphie. Lucy sat at the edge of the bed, looking at everyone with a cautious inquiring gaze.

Then the nurse told him that Dr. Freeman was coming in to see him.

"We can't be responsible for you," the doctor said when Bines insisted he was going, "if you don't stay for more observation."

"You should stay," Ralphie said.

"No, no – don't want you to be responsible for me – responsible for me – responsible for meself."

And he would answer no more questions, say nothing else.

Bines didn't stay in the wheelchair but got up and asked Ralphie to help him. It was strange to see that he was vulnerable.

"I want you to see if anyone is out by my truck," he said.

Bines waited near the door. Ralphie came in and told him that there was no one around his truck.

"You sure?" Bines said, and Lucy ran herself to check.

"No one's there," she said, coming back a moment later.

Bines nodded.

They started out across the parking lot, with Lucy rushing ahead to open the door and then coming back to help him to it.

"It's a miracle you're alive," Lucy kept saying, her face dazzling. "It's a miracle is all I can say."

Bines lay on the couch, and kept listening to the wind, with a cup of tea poured into an old mug resting on his lap.

"What time is it?" he said.

"Quarter to two," Ralphie said.

"Quarter to two," he repeated. His mouth looked

127

pensive now that his eyes were wrapped, and the wrapping was so spotless it looked out of place resting against Bines' hair.

"Quarter to two," he repeated again.

Ralphie went and looked out the window. The sky was clear. The stars dotted the sky and made a great canopy over the soundless trees and uprooted stumps of the clearcut. Some snow lay against these stumps, a fine clean powdered snow. A way around the bend the river was silent and the dark shape of the island Ralphie owned was just visible. He had been left the island by his father, and he had always thought that he would build a camp on it, but there was a dispute with the Indian reserve over fishing rights, and though Ralphie had hardly stepped on it he'd never considered selling it.

Bines touched the wrapping and turned his head as if to look Ralphie's way.

"How do you like William?" Bines said.

"Oh – I like him very much," Ralphie said, smiling innocently, the way he always did when he was genuine and wanted to show affection.

"Like him, do ya – don't think he's spoiled – spoiled, is he?"

"No," Ralphie said.

"I already got him to half-tie his own fly," Bines said. "That's not so bad, is it?"

"That's great," Ralphie said.

"I never touch him," Bines said, pointing a finger out

of the darkness. "You know, hit him or nothin – spose you thought I hit him?"

"No, of course not," Ralphie said.

"You didn't think that there?"

"No."

"Oh – well anyways – I was thinking about it, and thought you might have," Bines said.

It seemed that this was something which had worried Bines a good deal and now he was relieved. He reflected about something a moment.

"Don't treat him like my old man treated me," he said.

Ralphie couldn't answer. He only nodded silently.

"Tea's cold," Jerry said.

When Jerry was young, wearing mittens and Humphry pants, his father used to take him down to the old rink to get him to fight with boys from the rapids and elsewhere, boys sometimes four or five years older than he, for a quart of wine.

"Move under him – you're smaller than he is – when he throws a right go inside and counter with your left – that little cocksucker won't get ya – won't get ya – you hit like a mule," his father would say, maniacal in his own detachment from his son's plight, his half-bared head catching the stiff breezes and being pelted by sharp falling rain, mixed with snow.

"Won't get ya," Bines would nod, his lips trembling in the freezing rain, sliding on his rubber boots, "Won't get ya," his small hands flailing away, and yet like something natural to his nature his punches short and hard under the dim light from the crooked shed, where men who had wanted to intervene but were frightened in some way stayed inside, the quart of wine Digger had bet on being held in someone else's hand, and the sound of a truck throttling.

But no matter – no matter. It never mattered. He could not take the fear away. It was always there. Somewhere, like he had been hurt and lost a long time ago. As if a long time ago he wanted his father to hug him, and to say: "It's all right, Jerry – all right. You know what I'm going to do for you? You know where we're going to go? I betcha ya don't know – I betcha you don't."

And his mother would laugh and they would all laugh, and his mother would go too.

11

At 3:00 in the morning, Bines unwrapped his eyes in the back porch of his house. By that afternoon, the pain along his left side, and particularly in his left arm, had grown worse. Still he went into town. He parked his truck and moved slowly down the street to a small store, where he bought a copy of the local paper.

"Man Escapes Blast," he read.

He read the story about himself with difficulty, and felt good that people would say those things about him; that there was going to be a book on him as well. But then people had always said he was exceptional and Bines had always taken himself to be, and as with most men and women who have the belief that they are exceptional there is a certain inability to feel as much for others as they do for themselves.

"Although Mr. Bines is no stranger to us . . .," he read, and then he read the story about how his father had made him fight in the pulpyard against men when he was thirteen, and how he was not a stranger to his share of trouble. And the story finished up: perhaps he was "more sinned against than sinning." An expression Bines had never heard before, but he nodded with conviction and satisfaction when he read this, the same way he had when he was acquitted at his trial.

Now it was growing dark, and he waited to see his son whom he knew his mother had brought to town. When he saw the boy he moved across the street and into the park.

"Where you goin, Willie?" he asked.

"Meet mom," the boy said. And in fact Bines saw his ex-wife walking towards them at that moment.

She walked up to them and nodded. Her hair was red, and she had eyes that were pale blue. She wore a fawn-coloured kerchief that smelled of evening. In all ways she looked like a country girl in town.

"Look," Bines said, showing them the article.

"Yes," she smiled slightly, as if she were afraid. "I read it."

For some reason he was slightly disappointed in this. There was a picture of the camp on page two and he showed it to William.

"Come through the door, Willie," he said. "Through the door, almost blew my ears off."

Again his ex-wife smiled as if she were frightened, and looked at her son. Her face was covered in small transparent freckles. He was trying to make something up to her by showing her this article on him.

"What does this mean here?" he said, pointing to the quote.

"'More sinned against than sinning,'" she said, looking up at him again in consternation, and puzzlement, as the evening now smelled of snow and brown mud. It was as if she didn't want to tell him. He looked at her and smiled.

"What does it mean?"

In fact, he found out it meant exactly what she would want for herself, and what everyone seemed to want – even what Joe Walsh had seemed to want. To be more sinned against than sinning.

He shrugged when she told him.

"Is yer minister more sinned against than sinning?" he said.

"Of course," she said.

"But they would never say that about him – in fact, before he dies they will say just the opposite –"

He said this very calmly, but she knew he was upset with her for not liking this article. He took the paper suddenly and threw it in the garbage barrel a few feet away as if it were nothing important. He shrugged. "Don't matter anyways," he said. "Don't matter –

anyway just go to the drugstore for me – before it closes – just go over – eye drops – got a sore eye –"

His son looked up at him and then went cautiously over to the barrel to retrieve the article.

"Leave it be, Willie," he said. "Leave it be."

§

Bines wanted to give his boy a benefit. And in December – about the eighth – he went to Ralphie to ask him to help out.

Ralphie told him that they should try to have the benefit after Christmas – for it was too close to the season, and people were very busy – but that he could try to organize it through the Kinsmen some time in January.

"But you don't understand," Bines said, "I already told his mom we would have one – have one – already said he would. Maybe Adele could help out or something – Adele help out."

"I know she would," Ralphie said. "She'd help out in a minute – I know she would."

"I want to have him a benefit," Jerry said, and then he paused. "I want people to know I had him one – had him one. I want his mom to know it too –"

Jerry had told his wife and little boy about the benefit he and Ralphie were planning. Why he did this as early as November 18, before he had even asked Ralphie, and a day before his camp blew up, no one was certain. But then other things happened to take him away from it.

"What kind of benefit will it be?" his wife had asked.

"A big one," Jerry said, "I'll only have a big one – right, Willie?"

The little boy looked at him, his eyes as big as saucers, and smiled faintly holding a toy truck in his hand. His lips were pale blue, and there was a slight bluish tinge to his forehead. But Bines looked at this death in life very strangely – that is, almost hopefully.

"Here," he said, suddenly, hauling out a receipt from his parka. "I ordered you a book – a book – I went to the store and ordered you it. I asked the girl – girl at the store and she says 'order him a book on dinosaurs – kids love dinosaurs' – so I did. Getting ya a book on dinosaurs – they lived a long time ago – right here in the back yard maybe, though I don't know. Maybe you and I could go dig for some dinosaur bones some day – in the back yard there maybe – I don't know."

Ralphie however could not get people interested in the benefit on so short notice – not before January 17.

He told Bines to wait, and that in January he would make sure he had everything organized. He would have the Kinsmen's hall or the Lions Club, and they would have a fundraising benefit as Bines had seen them do for other children.

"Okay," he said. "Fine."

He shrugged and smiled, and took some Aspirin, just as his father had done twenty years before, for the pain.

He said nothing else about it again.

§

Some nights his wife would wake and Bines would be sitting in a chair in the other bedroom, with his boy.

She would wake up and feel his presence in the house.

"The medicine is making him sick," he whispered one night. "He's still got them bruises – and his hair isn't growing back like they said."

"That's all right. Dr. Lem told me it's only an antibiotic to clear up some infection; the chemotherapy is working. You have to go in January for that operation – so he wants everything cleared up."

Bines had been tested for bone marrow in September and the operation was finally scheduled for just after Christmas. Always her voice was uncertain as if she was trying to explain something unfathomable to him and was worried that he would not understand and get angry. She also felt indebted to him because of the bone marrow. And he knew this and hated it. Did she not think he would do it in a heartbeat? This angered him as he looked at her.

"That's just a little annoyance – you know they gave him a transfusion – the last time he was in. It's just a little annoyance – Dr. Lem said." He held his hand up.

And then, moving into the kitchen, he sat with his hands on his knees.

On the old oak table there was a Bible, and a vase of imitation daisies with huge plastic petals. Over in the corner there was a group of sloganizing plaques on the wall.

His wife came out and sat in the chair near him with her head down, as if she were waiting to be lectured. He looked at her a moment, ready to say something, but then he stopped. He did not know what to say to her anymore. So he said: "Read me a part from the Bible."

"The what?"

"Bible – read me a part –"

It was after 3:00 in the morning. The kitchen was dead quiet. The air was cold, and some snow had gathered about the outside window frame.

"Yer always telling me you're good on the Bible."

She picked the third marker from the back of the New Testament and looked down at it.

"Pick a part," he said again.

She was shivering, her arms were bare, and her legs trembled. When she started reading her voice shook and broke and was lost because of the presence of the man sitting off to the side with his bolt-black eyes resting upon her.

"'I am the true vine – and my Father is the husbandman; no one comes to the Father except by me.'"

She looked up. There were some cookies in the dish. He seemed distracted. He remembered how Willie liked those kind of cookies.

"Ya," he said, and he nodded silently. "That's good, though," he said, smiling. "That's good."

Ralphie had not seen Bines in two or three days when he got a call at his shop.

"I shouldn't tell you," Adele said.

"Tell me what?"

"Jerry wants you to go and bail him out."

"Of jail."

"Well, not out of church, Ralphie-face."

"What did he do?"

"Threw a table through a wall at the hospital."

"Why?"

"You'd have to ask the turbulent mind of Mr. Jerry Bines," Adele said. "Oh," she said almost as an afterthought, "he wants you to bring money, so you'd better not disappoint him – his friends are not allowed to."

Ralphie went to the police station and bailed Jerry out. And felt numb the whole time. It gave him a strange sensation that Jerry would ask this favour of him.

"I'll pay you back," Jerry said, as if he were worried that Ralphie would think badly of him.

"No – I mean don't worry about it. What happened?"

Jerry told him that no doctor wanted to take responsibility for his boy, that he had finally been scheduled to go to Halifax for tests, but they were now postponed, which meant the operation wouldn't take place until early February. He seemed to be very agitated about this.

"Well, I'm sure they are trying their best," Ralphie said.

"They're all frightened of taking responsibility for the boy. They didn't ever consider it was leukemia. At first they just thought it must've been me beating him."

Jerry said that all the doctors were frightened of the boy because of who he was.

"They all know who he is, and they're all scared something will happen to him. I demanded that we go today – to Ronald McDonald house – to Ronald McDonald house – demanded we go there now. But it's not scheduled up until the fourth of February – fourth – that's too late."

Ralphie again did not know what to say, so he only shrugged.

"They can mix my wife up with it – she puts her faith in things – in things," Jerry said.

"In what things?"

"I don't know – not the same things I do – different than me – than me."

The doctor he had wanted to see had gone on vacation and his son had to wait in the outpatient ward for over two hours. Jerry already had the boy's bag packed. No one had any idea why he was there and he became upset when they finally told him that Dr. Lem was not available, that there was no ambulance scheduled to take the boy to Halifax, and that Dr. Charing, who would perform the operation, was not available either.

"I'm sorry about it but I won't be laid a hand on," Jerry said.

"Well, who laid a hand on you?"

Jerry didn't answer. Then he looked at Ralphie, as if trying to atone for something. "I don't want to lose the boy," he said. "He's only small." And he turned away.

"I have to go back down to Lucy's and get William," he said. "He's all upset – just like his mom now. That's no good at all."

When Ralphie came home he sat down on the small chair in the living room.

"Do you know why I don't like him?" Adele said. She came into the room and looked down at him. He was lost in thought. His hair was turning white, and his whole life was filled with expectations that to him had not materialized.

"I don't know why you don't like him," he said, matter-of-factly. "Not at all."

"When I knew him he wasn't famous – not like he is now. His dad used to hold parties up at his house and Joe was still tilted then and used to go up. Jerry used to beat up the kids and take their money – he was a little snitch, and his father Digger used to hit on the old man – but Joe wouldn't hit him back because he was his sister's husband maybe or he had a plate in his head. Digger would wait until Joe got drunk and then throw a punch and knock him off the chair. He was built just like Joe – strong as a mule."

"So that was years ago – look how Jerry had to grow up," Ralphie said. "His father wasn't responsible for his actions. He had pain in his head all the time."

Adele sat down on the seat opposite him. In the pale light of afternoon she looked her age, like Rita had looked some fifteen years before.

But this is not what Adele had wanted to say.

She wanted to tell him about the tractor-trailer that was stolen, and Joe losing everything because of it.

"Oh, I don't think that was Jerry," Ralphie said.

He said this in the way every man or woman does when they choose not to want to know.

"Who put the finger on that tractor-trailer, Ralphie-face?"

Ralphie didn't answer.

"What lad in town would be brash enough to do that?"

Ralphie didn't say anything. He only looked up and then looked away.

"Who do you love more – me or Jerry Bines?"

"You," Ralphie said.

"Who put the finger on that tractor-trailer, Ralphie?"

Ralphie didn't answer.

The day was growing darker, panning out into one shadow with the moon over the trees lying down flat on its back.

"Who do you think you hurt when you talk of Jerry Bines as a hero?"

Ralphie didn't answer.

"Who wanted to see my sister graduate from university?"

"Joe."

"And that's the guy they suspected when they couldn't find their cigarettes."

Ralphie sat with his head down, a strange smile on his face.

"Who put the finger on those cigarettes, Ralphie? Who put the fuckin finger on that tractor-trailer?"

"He's all changed now – he's trying to change," Ralphie whispered. "Joe – Joe wouldn't mind him now, he'd help him."

"There is a dream about the most beautiful boy in the world being cold on the street – and you are in it – it was in the dream I had one night when you went up to see him at the hospital and I say to you in the dream, 'Don't look at him, don't pick him up, because as soon as you pick him up he changes and becomes something else.' That was a dream I had, Ralphie-face."

Ralphie didn't answer.

"It's his power that you like, Ralphie-face."

Ralphie didn't answer.

"There is trouble coming – I can tell." And she tilted her body over and reached into a stack of papers that were ready for the fire. She showed Ralphie a picture of Bines' camp. "Why did he blow this up?"

"Oh, he didn't blow it up," Ralphie said, in the tone of voice that suggested that someone had gone too far in their argument.

"Someone is on his way and Jerry doesn't want him using it – so he blows up his camp."

"That's the most ridiculous theory I've ever heard," Ralphie said, as a less perceptive person will always tout their rationality.

"Someone is coming and he doesn't want him using it. That's why he blew up his camp."

Ralphie didn't answer. He seemed to be cold and his beautiful hands trembled slightly, as if they were trying to find some bolt or screw or attachment to fix.

"What did you teach me, Ralphie?"

"I don't know."

"You taught me in calculus that everything is for a purpose, everything happens – a rock falls twenty storeys at an angle that laws of ten billion or hundred years says it must. That's what I put faith in when you lost your feasibility study – and the eighty thousand that went along with it. That's what I put faith in when our life went wrong – when Mommie and Joe died – why did Bines blow up his camp?"

"I don't know."

"That's what I put faith in – who fingered the tractor-trailer?

"I don't know."

"Who was Daddy trying to sober up?"

Ralphie didn't answer.

"Jerry – who everyone told him not to trust – who knew Dad had to pick up 120 thousand dollars' worth of cigarettes – who knew he was going to go to Saint John."

Ralphie lit a cigarette and looked out the window as if he were very interested in something outside.

It was not as if this was an unusual way for Adele to argue. She had argued like this for years – over matters far less consequential. And Ralphie pretended that all of these arguments were the same and not one new idea was ever explored. And to do this he looked out the window, and puffed on his cigarette.

"Who sent him a postcard – when he was in prison?" he said. "Who told me that they took care of him the year his mom died?"

Adele faltered, and looked about the room.

"And who loves this most beautiful child in the world – you don't want me to pick up? Whose family is the only family on the river ever to love him?"

Adele didn't answer.

There was a long silence.

"Loves that most beautiful child in the world –"

There was another silence.

"Because he is their own. And he's come home now – asking forgiveness –"

There was another silence.

"Looking for shelter."

There was another silence. Then Ralphie whispered: "Tired of being hunted down."

12

Nevin took the bus to Fredericton. It was a long dreary ride, and the bus stopped many times, to let off passengers or to pick up parcels. He was on his way to see his first wife.

After they reached McGivney Station he slumped into a depression.

It was fine to say to yourself you were going to meet someone and ask forgiveness for a cruelty you had done. It was another thing to actually do it.

He went along the old street where they had once lived, near the farmer's market, and felt himself shivering. All the memories of those youths who had grown up on popular songs of revolution and change, and used it to hurt and bully others until they themselves floundered into middle age and obscure dreams on windswept streets while the lights flickered on at dusk.

For nearly an hour he stood in the parking lot behind the apartment he and his wife had shared. Memories flooded him of her hanging out the clothes, or smiling at him when he came home.

Finally he went to the door and knocked. An old lady answered it, and he stared into the same kitchen he and his wife shared almost twenty years before. Except it looked much homier now with a great degree of quietude.

"I was looking for Gail White," Nevin said.

"No, I'm sorry, this is the wrong apartment. You could try upstairs."

Nevin nodded. "Okay, I'll do that," he said.

And he turned and walked along the street towards University Avenue.

With Nevin the compulsion to have a drink was almost always unbeatable. Sooner or later he would have to submit to it. And the idea of course was that he had already submitted to it, and the matter was settled. He took out his change purse – for he had always carried one – and looked through it. Besides the little miniature picture of Hadley, and an older picture of Vera, he had four dollars in change, which would give him a few draft at any rate.

He smiled at this, and he looked through every

pocket of his coat, not only for more money, but to make sure he had his return ticket.

The old tavern was gone with a new one in its place, and he sat down. Over in the corner a heavy-set man with a huge black beard and a worker's vest was looking at him.

It was Gail's brother. Nevin knew this instantly but the man didn't seem to know why he recognized Nevin.

"What'll it be?" the waiter said.

"Yes – just a minute," Nevin answered.

He went over to Donnie and sat down.

"Oh ya – Nevin – well, how are you?" Donnie said.

He put out his huge hand and held Nevin's gently and shook it up and down the way a man does who is hardly ever this formal.

Nevin was frightened that there would be abuse heaped upon him or scorn or ridicule for how he had treated Gail. But Donnie only said, "Boys it's been a long time since I seen you – where you been?"

"Oh, haven't been any place in particular," Nevin said. "Do you want a beer – I'll buy you a beer."

"Ya, sure – I'll have a beer," Donnie said, "and then I'll buy you one."

"No, just get me a pop," Nevin said. "What are you doing?"

"Oh, I work on tractor-trailers – work on them – probably be run over by the sons of whores some day." And he smiled. He took his beer and drank a sip and looked about as if he didn't know what to say.

"You a professor now I suppose or somethin like that."

"No, no, I'm nothin like that," Nevin said. He wanted to be derisive about professors and say that is why he couldn't be one, but Donnie only smiled at him kindly, and he found he could not.

"Oh, I was thinking of you just the other day –"

"When was that?"

"Oh, I don't rightly know," Donnie said, in the old-fashioned way, and smiled. "Oh, yes, it was the day I had to drive the grader down to Hampton – what day was that?"

Nevin shrugged, and lay his huge mittens on the table before him.

Donnie looked about again and then yawned and looked at his boots. They were frayed and torn and untied.

"Well boys I don't know she's some bad now this economy," he said, looking up.

"Yes, it is," Nevin said.

"The country is more or less a ghost now," Donnie said.

"That's true," Nevin said.

There was a pause.

"More or less useless as a country now," Donnie said holding his glass and drinking, while he looked around the room.

"So, are you married?" Nevin asked.

"Oh ya – married now, a boy and two girls."

He cupped the glass in his huge hands so it was almost hidden.

"Where's Gail?" Nevin said. He said it in a way that startled him. He held his breath after he said it.

Donnie took his big thumb and pointed it sideways.

"Oh, she's just here –"

"She married too?" Nevin said, after a pause.

"Oh ya – married – married a boy from home – Furlong – George Furlong – no, you wouldn't know him," Donnie said, shaking his head at himself.

"I'm glad," Nevin said, although secretly he was disappointed.

"Oh ya – well, she's doing all right you know – you too married now?"

Nevin shook his head. "No, no – I'm not married."

It was growing dark. The snow was hard on the street, the lane lying brown and salted in small neat heaps, and the lights were on above the wires, shining golden on the snow.

Nevin followed him outside and stood beside him a moment.

"Do you know where I can find her?" he said.

"Who? Oh, Gail – well, she'll be home now," he said. And he told Nevin where she lived.

"You need a drive?" he said.

"No," Nevin said, "I can walk."

And he started out briskly, with the wind and the cold in his face.

The house was across the river. The driveway was

ploughed to the stones, and an old hockey net sat inside the open door of the garage.

The closer he got to the door the more nervous he became, until his whole body shook.

"She will laugh in my face," he thought. "She will laugh and then spit in my face."

But he was propelled not by his courage but by some other aspect of his nature. He took off his hat and held it in his hand, and knocked.

The door was opened by a little girl.

Nevin looked at her. A little over three feet highp with big brown eyes and her whole head a mat of tiny curls.

"Mommie, it isn't Patty – it isn't Patty –"

"Well, who is it?" he heard.

"It's me," Nevin heard himself saying.

Gail came to the top of the stairs and looked down at him, bending her head down to make out his face.

"It's me," Nevin said, smiling slightly, "Nevin."

"Nevy –" she said.

He had not been called Nevy in twenty years.

"Yes," he said, "it's me."

He stood at the door and she came down the stairs.

It was, to Nevin, as if they had said goodbye earlier that morning.

"Thea," she said gently to the little one, "don't block the door." And she smiled.

She was now forty years old, but to him she was exactly as she had been.

She had three children and it was right at supper time.

The baby was in the highchair, with a big plastic bib on, which made his face look very chubby, and covered with red spaghetti sauce. The older boy sat at his own table in the hallway, drawing. There was something reserved about him that Nevin did not like – he did not know why. Perhaps it was only because he was no longer a child but a little boy, something he took very seriously.

Perhaps it was just because Nevin was nervous. He put his mittens in his pockets.

Have you had your supper?" she said.

"Oh, I've just got a minute," Nevin said. "I was in town and saw Donnie – so I just thought I'd drop over."

"Oh, yes – well – you were where? Up at the university?" she said, somewhat cautiously, as if she didn't want to intrude on his intellectual doings.

"Yes," Nevin said, sitting down in a chair, "on business – so I just thought I'd come over and see you – I mean see about how you were."

She smiled and sat down.

"You just missed my husband," she said. "He's gone to work – just went out the door –"

There were shouts of children playing road hockey on a side street and far away a train shunted with a thud that was muffled by the snow.

"It's good to see you," she said. "I often wondered where you were now – and what you were doing. I mean, almost every week I think about you."

Instantly Nevin thought of making up a story to impress her. But he only said, "I wanted to see you for a long, long time."

After a moment she said, brightly, her eyes shining, "You didn't know that I ran after you – after you went around the corner – did you?"

"Oh no, I didn't know that," he said, and he tried to make it sound light-hearted but it didn't sound that way. Then he cleared his throat. "If I had known that – maybe I would have turned back," but he thought he had said this too flippantly.

She smiled gently and smoothed her hands on her apron and looked about the room, but averted her eyes somewhat.

"I wanted to find you for a long time," Nevin said. "I did not know where you went – where –"

"Oh well," she said simply. "We were both young." She looked at him. "I mean, we can't blame ourselves – it was so long ago now."

"Oh no – no," Nevin said, "I don't blame myself about anything."

She smiled. There was some powder on her chin, and she wiped it away. Then when she turned to the baby, when he saw her slight back and the angle of her head so he could see her small neck and the medallion's chain clasped to it, he said, almost humbly: "That's not true – I've always blamed myself – I always thought – not always, but in the last five or six years, that I should never have gone away – that I always loved you – that I always loved you and –"

She turned to him and her eyes seemed startled with hurt, and then suddenly she reached over and put her fingers to his lips.

"Shhh," she said, and her eyes filled with tears.

It was as if he had gone around the corner but had decided to come back, and all those years – all those years had never passed or mattered in any way.

"I've always loved you," he said, through her fingers. "Why did I belittle you – why did I belittle –"

"Shhh," she said, and smiled. "Shhh."

He left an hour later to catch his bus.

He was out on the street and he looked up at the stars, and felt a kindness in the cold air, a warmth in the battered naked trees, and he didn't bother to put on his hat.

The boy came out with his jacket unzipped and his boots on.

"Here," he said, and running to the edge of the driveway he handed Nevin two peanut-butter cookies, which were still warm from the pan. "Mom says to give these to you for your trip on the bus."

And then he nodded and ran back to the house, turning suddenly at the door to wave goodbye.

13

It was now the middle of December.

In the darkness a man of medium height and build, about fifty to fifty-five with greying hair and a sharp, somewhat impressive face, with very pale blue eyes that were somewhat sunken into his head, made his way along a street in town. He had a false ID and two hundred dollars in jewellery in his pocket that he himself had calculated to be worth much more. His name was Gary Percy Rils.

He had been wanted on a Canada-wide warrant for the last six months, for escaping custody and a murder committed in Sudbury, and though summer had been fine, now he was cold and tired. There was over a bootful of snow on the ground. He wore shoes and thin grey socks, and suit pants that the wind cut through.

He was the darker square of the jigsaw, the most oppressive in his disregard for the life of others, and the most vindictive in his sense of self-perpetuation.

He moved into the derelict lot and sat for a while on an oil barrel. Seeing a police car drive by he gamefully waved to the constable, who nodded back, and, lighting a cigarette, looked back over his shoulder at some noise on the road above him. The small trees that were once here had disappeared. The earth had the smell of cinder and wet snow. He had just walked through the woods about one half-mile and it had frightened him.

In all ways over the last twenty-five years he had become a city boy – and yet something compelled him to believe that this was where to be. He had had no idea an hour ago that he would make it here and be sitting in this old derelict lot. But this is where he now was.

Across the street a tiny light shone out from the house, and a wind started. The sky was brutally clear, the streetlights glimmered.

He had been Buddy's friend since they met in Dorchester in 1976, and this is where sanctuary would be for a while. He made his way across the street and knocked, quickly kicking the snow from his flat, soaking shoes.

The knock was answered by a shuffle inside, as if a disturbance had been interrupted, and finally the door opened. A soft light shone on his face.

"Oh," Alvin said. He said nothing more for a

moment, and it was as if he were wondering whether or not he could close the door and lock it before the man put his forearm in, which he had started to do.

Rils' face was one of those faces which, in the light of a room, demonstrated a total invariable of expression. It was simply cold.

"Hello, Alvin," Gary Percy said as he came in. His fine hair was soaking and stuck in three separate ropes against the back of his neck. Sticking from his jacket were two or three small boughs, which he had placed inside to keep warm.

He glanced about the room. Over in the corner, curled up and watching him, while she smoked a cigarette – like young people do, with the affectation of someone older and wiser – was Lucy. She had been in bed for three or four days, as she was every month at this time, and was now just coming around.

The man nodded in her direction, and the faint flicker of a smile passed over his face. Frances hobbled in from the other room, and looked at him. She had a sore ankle from where Alvin had kicked it. For his part he hadn't meant to kick her but he had gambled away some money of theirs on the machines and everyone at the tavern – or those he put the most stock in – had teased him, and when he came home he took it out on her.

Alvin had been walking around the room, finishing up the beer left over from the night before, when the man knocked, and he was telling the children that they were all to go out and get jobs. When the knock came on the door he had thrown a shirt over his back to hide his stump – which he hardly showed to anyone outside the family.

When Gary Percy came in, Alvin looked cautiously at his daughters and said nothing. But his face looked as if he had just taken a hit in the mouth.

However, regaining his composure, though his hand was trembling as he held it out for the man to take, he smiled as if a trick had just been played on someone and he had been a part of it, and thought that it was a fine thing.

"How did you make it here?" he said in a voice a little too enthusiastic, so he tried to look suspicious at the same time.

"I've been around here for a month," the man said, "though they don't know." And he tossed his head as if to indicate the police. But this was a lie, though it didn't matter.

Lucy caught what she always caught about men when they came to the house, and which she had caught since she was a little girl, that is, whether these men were weak or strong. And she could see by the way her father looked that this man was strong and even more so than Jerry Bines. She had known this before.

She sat up and looked at him. From far away she looked like her cousin Adele, except there was no great softness of her features that enhanced her looks. She was beautiful or would be, there was no doubt about that.

Rils sat down on the edge of a chair and looked about. The wind blew outside and the old house seemed to crack and move. The lights themselves flickered slightly.

"Where's Jerry?" he asked, and again Lucy looked over at him cautiously, and lit another cigarette.

"I haven't seen him," Alvin said.

"Tell him I want him," he said, and he glanced over at Frances, who stood in the same position she had when he came in.

"Well, I don't know where he is."

Then Alvin told him that Jerry spent most of his time now with Ralphie Pillar – hanging around with the judge's son. Gary Percy said nothing about this for a moment. "Has he got religion or money?" he said finally.

"I think he had a little of both," Alvin said, suddenly realizing disgust at Bines.

The man shrugged, but his small eyes glittered in an immobile darkness. All the children, who were sitting in small rows on the stairway, all those blonde and brown-headed little girls, who had been born in this household and were now waiting for Christmas to come, watched him. They all noticed the cheap watch on his wrist, because its imitation gold glittered somewhat.

"He might be here tomorrow night," Frances said.

"Oh, he still designs to come here, does he –" Gary Percy said. And the whole family laughed, even the little girls on the steps.

Lucy then stood and walked by him with her blanket wrapped about her, because she was almost naked under it.

She turned and looked back over her shoulder for a second, and then went upstairs to her room.

The thing was she had no love for Gary Percy Rils. She thought only of warning Jerry Bines.

Lucy got dressed later and went out through the old back hallway which slanted, and down the back stairs with a door at the bottom. She stole away in the dark and crossed the picket fence.

She went to Ralphie's shop and looked through the glass. There was no one there. The stars were out and it was cold.

Boys on the street whistled to her.

"Hey Luc—cy," they said.

"Piss off," her answer was.

She made her way through the small gate at the side of the brick shop and along a narrow street grown more narrow with snow until she reached the highway, and then she cut across the graveyard in a hurry.

In ten minutes she was at a small house above the

tracks where a group of boys, and one or two girls, were sitting smoking and talking.

"Where's Jerry?" she asked.

No one had seen him.

She waited in the house a moment because she was cold. Ice had formed on the window outside.

Then she turned and walked back down over the hill. It was after eleven at night and she had no idea what to do. Her boots made a soft echo of late night as she walked along the street, and the lights in the houses were out.

When she got back to her own street she saw Jerry's truck coming in the other direction slowly. He flashed his lights and she ran up to him.

"Gary is here," she said.

He nodded and looked out the window.

She got into the truck and he began to drive.

"I have to get him off the river," he said. "Do you know where there's any money?"

"No."

"Where is he?"

"At the house."

"Well, he can't stay there – Alvin'll get drunk and start blabbing it all over town – I have to be away but I'll be there when I can – when I can."

He left her at the corner, and, turning his truck quickly about, he drove off.

§

The man who had been at the camp with Andrew came back with them to the house for breakfast.

It was now July. The screen door let in a breeze that was almost forlorn. The street was hot though, and the great shrubs had turned brown at their tips.

Andrew was at the age where he was beginning to discover that intellectual beliefs did not always match action and that sins were sometimes overcome by personal attributes.

When he thought back to that night at their camp, and the wind and rain blowing across the thousands of puddles that filled and dotted the muddy roadway, he remembered Jerry Bines more than anyone else, and his handshake that seemed at once so powerful and vulnerable. The boy also had gone downtown to find a strap for his watch that was just like Bines' — but he couldn't find one. This was because the watch belonged to another age and another time, an age that was being swept away and replaced by a new age. Jerry Bines had belonged to that former age.

Bines had blown up his camp so Rils couldn't use it. He knew he was coming. He had known it for two months or more. He kept a shotgun in the house, loaded at all times. He knew Rils might follow him, so he did not go back to his wife's house except late at night.

What had happened at Jerry's camp? He went to set off the propane and it blew him backwards through the door. That night back in September when he came to their camp – that was the first night that he knew that Rils was coming.

Going through the camp door had made him lame in his left arm, bleed in his left lung.

He hid it as well as he could and for most of the time he stayed at home. Once he set up a bear trap in the back porch and wired his shotgun so it would go off if anyone opened the door. Then he would make phone calls to his wife.

"How's Willie?" he would whisper.

"Is that you, Jerry?"

"I want you to take the boy and go over to Fredericton to live with your sister."

"I can't do that, Jerry, they want nothing to do with us – they disowned me –"

"When did they disown you – disown you?"

"When I married you. They don't want to look at the boy, they don't speak to me."

If Christ had shed a drop of blood for every sin in the world, as Andrew believed, he must have shed a pint and a half for Jerry Bines. The whole idea, as he heard while busying himself with his Nintendo game that July morning in the small quiet house in the middle of a subdivision, of the bear trap and the shotgun being wired was worth an enormous amount of blood.

He had gone to his catechism priest to ask him about this.

"A drop of blood," the priest said, "for every sin."

"But there is a whole bunch of sins," the boy said. "A whole lot of them."

"So," the priest said, "now you know how much Jesus suffered."

"I can't understand it, we only have a few dozen pints of blood or something like that there – I mean *don't* we?"

"Oh yes, but now you're trying to reason with God. That's like the man who never thinks of Christ but reasons with God when times get bad and asks questions." And the priest smiled at his own answer, which increased his self-esteem as light came into the basement of the church.

§

Rils had been waiting in Alvin's house. He hardly moved from the upstairs bedroom where they had put him. But once in a while when someone came up those stairs he would say: "Jerry."

The person would pass on, or say something in a quiet voice to assure him it was not, and he would be quiet again. He had no money except for the jewellery, so he had given it to Alvin to sell for him at the tavern. Alvin, of course, to please him, had told him he had never seen such fine jewellery. There were a few stubby rings and an old watch and two bracelets with the name D. Henniker and the date 1982 on one. The other one was a tainted gold piece that had a broken clip, and which had dangled over Rils' fingers when he handed it over.

Snow was falling against the old slanted roof in big wet sleepy flakes. The road outside was indistinguishable from the rest of the landscape, and only identifiable by the cars that now and then cut a track through on their way into town. A huge ship lay off to the left with its deck lights giving a faint glimmer, as if it were a mile or more away.

In the room Alvin had put him in, there was a pile of boxes in the corner, a torn magazine or two, an old pink necklace lying on a dust-covered table, and a grade-six mathematics book with the cover torn and marked with an orange crayon. He spent the day staring out the window and smoking cigarettes. At nightfall he would come downstairs. "Call him," he would say.

"I have," Alvin would say, twisting his body about in the chair. "He's not home."

"Well, when will he be home?"

"I don't know. His wife said he was seeing to his boy – so he'll be around."

"What's wrong with his boy?"

"I don't know –"

Rils was becoming more impatient with this.

"Well, I'm going to sell your jewellery," Alvin said.

"Don't sell the bracelets for less than two hundred dollars apiece, or the watch," Rils said. "No one could get stuff like that around here."

"I know," Alvin said, looking up at him cautiously, "but we'll see what I can get."

Whenever Rils mentioned Jerry he would say "he." He would start with "he" – or in the middle of a sentence about something obscure the pronoun "he" would come into play, and everyone would know he was speaking about Jerry.

Gary Percy Rils asked if Lucy could get him a shotgun.

"No," she said, "but probably Jerry could."

"He probably could, ya – probably could." And the very fact that Jerry could get him a shotgun seemed particularly disturbing to him.

Lucy looked at him quietly.

"I will be gone for a little while, and you won't see me," Jerry had said, "I just have things to do – in a little while I'll be back."

So she waited patiently, listening for his truck in the middle of the night.

14

Bines had gotten home and kept his grandmother upstairs. He moved about the house like he was on his tiptoes, going from window to window.

He would never be included into that group of men and women which he deceived himself into thinking that he could belong to. He had almost willed himself to be with them. Almost had succeeded in making a good impression.

He went and sat in the porch. His whole left side was numb and his eyes were sore.

"It don't matter," he thought. "Don't matter."

He did not like Rils, and though he believed he was not frightened of him he could see Rils in his mind's eye.

"If I don't get him off the river he'll end up killing some-one," he thought.

For some men, to think of murder and blood would be horrid and preposterous. For Bines it was simply a matter of fact. And he knew also Rils would pick on someone weak –

"Someone like Willie or Gram," he thought suddenly, and he threw his right arm out and a lamp went crashing into the wall. When he stood he staggered.

"What's wrong?" his grandmother asked. "Derry – Derry – Derry – Derry!"

"Nothin, Gram – you stay up there."

He took out the bottle of Aspirin he had in his pocket and he chewed a few of them. He felt strangely angered. He realized that he couldn't be admitted to the hospital. He feared that Rils would come after his wife and child.

He went into the living room and sat in the chair that Ralphie had first seen him in two months before.

"Whether she wants to go or not," he said, thinking of his wife, "she and the boy will have to go somewhere – get them off the river – get them somewhere."

He put the cap back on his bottle of Aspirin and placed it into his vest, the way one would place a pocket-watch.

He had gone to visit Vera every day for the last two weeks. But she was frightened of him, and Ralphie was also. He did not understand why they would be but they were. Still he clung to the idea that they were not, and that everything would resolve itself.

"I got him the chairs," he thought. "That's good though – that's good."

And he nodded and looked about the room.

He stood up and put his parka on and looked outside.

When he was young his father and he would go out to the Salvation Army for Christmas dinner. Now that it was the third week in December he thought of this. He thought of what would happen to Willie if he was no longer here.

"I am the true vine – no one comes to the Father except by me," he remembered suddenly.

It was strange to have been told that. He had never been told anything like that before.

And suddenly he picked up the shotgun and blew a hole in the wall.

He left the house and went to visit Vera. It was for one thing only. He wanted her help in changing the boy's name. To make the boy anonymous in the place he had to live. Bines had been thinking about this for months but Vera thought that it had all come about because of her positive influence over him.

"It'd be better for Willie if his name was changed," he said.

Of course it would," she said. "He should really have his mother's name.

"Why don't you write down for me what you can

168

about your feelings for your wife and child," she said, "and also about your father. I think if you did that then I might be able to help you out – well, at least we might be able to get some feeling for what is going on."

"It'd be better for Willie," he said, "better if his name was changed."

That is all he said.

"You came from a dysfunctional family," Vera said, looking at him seriously.

"I don't know – don't know that there," Bines said.

Vera took the time, over three hours, to explain to him exactly where she thought he had come from.

Bines sat listening to this. Yes, it was all true, in a way. And he had never met a person like Vera before, who was so sure of herself when it came to someone else. He was only certain that in a way it was true.

And it was at this time that Bines, who was beset by pain in his left side, which he tried to hide even from himself, wrote his own story.

Vera published it later as part of her text, almost verbatim.

I was born in 1963. And there was a storm. Dad brought the horse up to put my mom in the sleigh. Then we went across the river. At the time there wasn't a bridge until you went five miles or more and the car won't go in a storm –

Some people were born in the hospital that night but I was born in the sleigh by Dr. Hennessey. My father was three sheets to the wind at the time as far as I was told about it. And had a big party. That he asked people to see me. Like the three wise men. (ha)

My old man was wounded in Korea and had a plate in his head that was as big as a saucer.

I think he was scared for my mom at the time, and didn't know what road to take or what to do.

And to please Vera he wrote:

I come from a dysfunctional family. I got mixed up in a lot a trouble.

I liked to hurt people for a long time. I was that way.

My mother was Joe Walsh's sister. And she was the prettiest girl my old man said about it.

I used to sing for men who came to the house. And I could walk across the table filled with wine bottles and ketchup and not touch one – and I had a trick where I could jump to the counter and get a beer out of the fridge and come back, without touching the floor. That was my best trick in those days.

I have a little boy who is sick. And now I see.

The story went on for another three pages, written in big looping handwriting with words misspelled, crossed out, and written over.

And when Bines brought this story to her he was very pleased – to please her.

One of the words he had written and crossed out and rewritten was "unconditional" because this is what Frances had said to him about his love for his father. But since he never mentioned the word "love," Vera took this to mean that his family didn't love – and that love was replaced by the violence of a domineering father. Which proved her case in a way about the things she at this moment believed – that the idea of love comes with being able to articulate love, which to Vera was part of the prominent lexicon of progressive thought.

§

But, the man told Andrew, slowly and by degrees, something happened. And Bines did not speak to Ralphie in the same way – that selfless way he had of atoning for himself.

"Look," he said to Ralphie one afternoon, "if you dislike the mill – if it pollutes us – I can get some dynamite and you can blow a few pipes up. That will shut it down for a month or so. We can go there tonight."

Ralphie was too amazed to say anything. He sat in his shop with his lips pressed together. Yet with Bines standing over him, he felt that this was some kind of a test. He did not know how this was, but he saw the cold sheets of snow on the roof of the building across the street – and when a moment ago he had been delighted to look out the window, now the atmosphere had changed to a drab and sunless afternoon.

There was silence as Bines waited for an answer.

"Well, it's a suggestion you should think of," Bines said. "Think of — if people do things to you, do things to them. That's not my rule, that's God's rule or somethin, isn't it?"

He seemed angry, so Ralphie didn't press him. But he had begun to see something, like the other side of a leaf, and the curious patterns therein.

The next afternoon Bines came back and said that he had not been thinking right – that he missed Joe Walsh – and he smiled again in the same selfless way, and Ralphie felt relieved. He said that he was pressured by something, and had to think things through. And before when he had to think things through he often went to Joe Walsh and they would talk.

His voice had a kindness in it – and Ralphie only smiled slightly, as if he was afraid he might have said something wrong.

But Bines no longer conferred respect over "important topics" such as the environment. When once he listened to Ralphie, now he no longer was the same. And Ralphie was frightened to argue with him, and Bines knew this.

"I don't agree," he would say calmly when Ralphie was explaining something.

"You don't?"

Bines would shrug and turn away, while Ralphie would become flustered and smile.

Ralphie would sit at home trying to think of how to get about this – how to avoid Bines' arguments without getting into trouble.

And when he looked at Adele, he knew that she sensed this.

He was enmeshed now in Bines' power. In the dark bolt-black eyes.

This side of Bines' nature seemed to have come through.

A new fact began to emerge. Bines was jealous of Ralphie's other friends.

"Why do you hang around with them?" he would say. "They wouldn't do anything for ya – anything for ya –"

"I just play bridge with them on Saturday nights."

"Ya, bridge – well – they'd do nothin for ya."

One of the men Ralphie played bridge with was the man who took out Andrew's mother. And he remembered both Ralphie and Bines at this time. He remembered Bines driving past them one night when they were leaving the rec centre after a game of bridge – a game Ralphie played exceptionally well.

Bines made a U-turn near the garage and came into the lot.

"What are you doing?" he said to Ralphie.

Ralphie smiled and looked about. The sky above them was black and empty – and pitiless in knowing all the things we do not know.

"I just had a game of cards," Ralphie said.

Bines looked at him, then at the other men.

"I'll see you tomorrow," Ralphie said to Bines, as if to appease him.

But Bines just drove off, scattering ice in the dark.

Andrew did not care so much about this anecdote at first, but slowly, like all anecdotes about Bines, it had a peculiar aspect to it which showed the total character.

Andrew had learned all of this from the man: Bines had struggled to ease the pain in his left arm by taking Aspirin all the time.

Then he went to meet Rils. He arrived in a snowstorm and came into the room. Now that he was here, Rils was almost shocked to see him.

"Where were you?" he said.

"Busy," he said.

Gary Percy Rils, who Bines had first met in Calgary.

"Damn stupid to meet him –" Bines often said.

Rils had always in a way been Bines' provider when he was out west, and therefore Bines was obligated to help him. He was obligated to help him also because Bines was a powerful man, and this made *him* a powerful man, and those at the prison were watching and waiting to see what would happen.

"I can get ya off the river," Bines said, sitting down. "But I can't promise ya nothing."

"Ya, well, I want to go back out west – it's no fun here," Rils said.

"No fun – no, don't suppose it is," Bines said. "Don't suppose it is –"

Bines' look had changed from when Lucy last saw

him. Neither Vera nor Ralphie would recognize his look now – it was filled with hatred. His eyes were bolt-black and filled with darkness, which he must have delighted in. His expression was one of fundamental nonlife.

Rils did not look at him, however. He took on the aspect of bored disinterest in what Bines was saying. "I need a shotgun, I need a walkie-talkie, I need a scanner. I need a coat and boots and hat – I want a knife."

"Sure," Bines said. "Ya'll be well-camouflaged with that –"

"I can't go downtown without a shotgun," Rils said, staring at Lucy.

"No, you shouldn't go walking around town without one. That's no good, is it?"

Rils looked at him quickly.

"Ya can't have my shotgun – but I'll see about one," Bines said. "See if I can get you one."

He said nothing more while Rils told his story of being in Kingston penitentiary.

The only problem now was money, could Bines get him some money.

"I don't know if I can get ya no money," Bines said.

But there was all this jewellery that he had. He had a thousand dollars' worth of jewellery – some of it was broken but most of it was good, and he would give it to Bines for six hundred dollars.

"Don't want it," Jerry said.

Sparks flew out of a chimney two or three houses down and snapped off in the air.

"A bargain – a bargain," Rils said, his voice carrying a tone of being stung.

"Don't want it," Bines said.

"Don't trust me?"

"Don't want it."

"Why don't you – I was your friend when you needed one – I was there when you needed me!"

"Don't want it."

Bines had met him in Calgary. For when you go anywhere, in the middle of the night, who do you go to but to those who will have you.

Alvin had been going back and forth carting things to Rils and the old dog followed him up and down stairs, and now sat wagging its tail at the door. It would hobble back downstairs when Alvin went, clicking its long nails on the tile. Alvin doted on it and fed it toast and jam and called it "sugar foot." And no matter how deeply it slept, once Alvin left the room it would lift itself up and hobble behind him, only to lie down again where Alvin sat.

That the old dog did this, hopping along on its lame feet and wagging its matted tail, looking up shamefully from one person to another as if trying to find a human it could understand, bothered Bines. That is, he could not stand to think that Rils would torment Alvin in front of his old lame dog, or the dog in front of Alvin.

Bines glanced over at Lucy and then at Alvin as Rils told a joke that was not so much off colour as childish.

Rils said he wanted to go by Christmas eve – but he had a few people to take care of, and some money to collect. "Christmas eve," Rils said. "That'll give us time."

Jerry tossed his head to one side and looked at the dog, who pitifully looked up at him thumping its tail.

Downstairs Alvin begged Bines to take him away.

"He can't stay here," Alvin said. "You have to take him – he's your friend – your friend – your friend." Alvin was close to tears and it was sad to see him crying in front of his children. Hazel stood behind him now, and could feel his legs trembling as he tried to smile. The old dog came over and sat near them, and gave a sad whine when it yawned.

Bines sighed and looked at Lucy. She too seemed to be worried, because the man upstairs was crazy. "He keeps talking about going out and killing an old woman or two – he says the world would be better off without a few old women. Or about getting the Pillars back. I don't know why he talks like that for," she said. "And we have a house filled with little kids here."

"If he touches anyone in town, I'll kill him," Bines said as if to reassure them.

"Well, that's all right for you to say – but it's us who'll be dead," Alvin said. "Jesus – we have little girls here,"

Alvin whispered. "I might turn him in is what I might do."

"No," Bines said. "Go get him – tell him to come with me."

Bines once again felt the power of his own personality surge through him because of what he had just said. But he also had nowhere to take Rils.

He had burned his camp for one reason only – so he would have no hiding place to offer. Now, to protect others, he felt he must find one.

Rils made Bines wait as he argued about leaving.

"No, I don't want you to go – it isn't me," Alvin said, "but you'd be safer with Jerry."

They came down the stairs twenty minutes later with Alvin leading the way, pale as a sheet and carrying two teacups in his hand to take into the kitchen, like a man who doesn't want some guest and makes the appropriate gesture to clean up in front of him when he has hope enough in his leaving.

Rils' expression had changed. He kept looking at Bines one moment and then looking away abruptly. Whenever Bines glanced at him he would notice Rils' eyes flit past him, as cold in their blueness as Bines' eyes ever were.

It was a look of absolute certainty of his betrayal at the hands of others, and instead of making him afraid, it gave him a frightening inquisitorial appearance, as if he were keeping score.

Bines called Rils Percy – a term of affection only a few people maintained with him.

And they left and walked out into the iron-smelling snow.

Their first falling out had been over the tractor-trailer, the man said, and now they had come to the second falling out – as soon as they got outside you could feel it between them.

The snow was coming out of the dark; the lumber sat off along the wharf, covered by snow. All the buildings were dark, their slanted roofs casting shadows on the white earth, as it was when Jerry was a little boy.

The argument came because Mr. Rils wanted to rob Mr. Pillar – that was the statement given by Lucy Savoie to Constable Petrie, in her meeting with him on January 3. The idea Jerry had was to get Rils some money, and to get him off the river. But he pretended there was nothing in Ralphie Pillar's shop that they could possibly steal. "Who am I to be interested in computers," he scoffed.

He pleaded ignorance of all the new world that was fast coming upon him to save Ralphie.

"Computers are worth a lot – computers are worth a lot," Gary said. "We could take half a dozen or so."

They went out into the snow, toward the truck, and became at that moment figures of some greatness, said the man. You can still almost see their breath in the dark, as the chimney smoke bit away.

Perhaps, the man said, Jerry was displeased that he was protecting those whom he now felt he would never belong to.

Perhaps he was displeased that, in actual fact, he was risking his own child to protect all of them who were at that moment asleep in their beds.

Why did they become figures of some greatness? the boy asked.

Because, the man said, they had become combatants in a life and death struggle, both deciding in breath and brain, more glorious than all the computers that had ever existed, their chances for one more day.

They went into the snow.

They got into the truck and drove away.

"I want to stay at your camp," Rils said.

"Don't have a camp," Bines answered. "Something happened – it burned."

Rils looked at him a moment, and then looked away.

They turned along the road, and drove outside of town.

"You can stay in my grandfather's barn," Bines said, after a long silence. He knew from that moment Rils had become his problem once again.

He left Rils in his grandfather's barn. Although Vera's research was done Jerry had to visit her once again.

Coldly self-sufficient, she had no idea he would come back and want to revise the story he wrote. He went to her office. To her this was a terrible imposition. She told him politely that she was very busy.

"Good," he smiled. "Busy – keep you out of trouble."

She looked up from her desk and nodded. "This is Christmas, it's always the worst time of year –"

"Ya," he said, "worst time – right – worst time."

"There's more family violence during Christmas than at all other times during the year," she said.

"Well, that's no good."

"No, it isn't," she said, in a slight voice of reprimand. "So anyway –" she paused, and nodded to someone outside her office door, which made Jerry turn slightly.

Jerry nodded at the person outside her door and looked back at her, and Vera got up and closed the door.

"Jerry, you don't need to come here every day."

"I didn't know I did."

"Well, I mean almost every day. I have serious work to do."

"Well," Jerry said, "I was thinking that if I'd get my story – there are things I would change – about it. I didn't get it right all the time – and –"

"Oh," Vera said, startled. "That. Well, I don't know where it is."

"Oh," Jerry said. "Ya lose it – lose it, did ya? I could write you another one – lose it?"

"No, I've not lost it. I'll look for it and send it along to you. I'm not trying to steal your story, Jerry."

"Steal my story –" Jerry nodded, almost embarrassed. "Why in fuck would anyone want to do something like that?"

It was growing dark on the street. His life had been nothing. His first wife was now a stripper in a bar in Calgary. His second wife had left him and to him Vera was someone almost untouchable, a part of the world he would occasionally glimpse and swipe at, like a cat at an ascending bird.

He still wanted to explain something. He didn't know why. And Vera sensed this.

"You must have hated your dad very much," Vera said.

"Oh, no," he said, his eyes shining, "I never did."

But he knew at that moment that she simply did not believe him.

"I never did," he said. "Never did."

"That's a natural reaction," Vera said. "You just have to realize that he's no longer worth protecting."

Bines looked at her. It seemed as if the very things he had wanted to make her see had been mistaken or misconstrued. The chasm between them had grown not lessened.

"What you want to protect," she said, "is the male line, that's all. But when the truth gets said it's always painful – especially when you discover it does not agree with your former notions."

"I have no notions," Bines said.

"Well, you certainly have some idea that you told on someone – and you don't like it. You probably always protected your father – your mother probably protected him as well. It's natural now to feel guilt."

Suddenly he realized he was being used for something much more complex than he ever realized. He never would understand this fully, and would go into the dark groping for it.

"Why do you want your boy's name changed?" she said.

"I don't know," Bines said. "Seems like a good idea."

"You want to get rid of your father's name," Vera said. "You want to stop the bleeding – that's why –"

And she smiled that certain smile that was present one moment and gone the next. A smile that was always controlled and said that the truth of the moment was to her the truth of all time.

All of her life Vera had gone from one religion to another asserting herself as its principal devotee. All his life Bines was searching for some notion of God, without ever having a concept of why he was.

Chekhov once wrote about a kiss, how it altered a soldier's life, how it made him dream of a rendezvous with someone he never knew. How he travelled back later only to see the faded emptiness of the house, the absolutism of reality.

Bines had brought Vera a present that visit.

"I almost forgot," he said, as he took it out of his parka.

"I can't take this," she said.

"Oh, it's nothin –" he said. "Christmas – for Christmas."

He was angered that she did not want it. He might too have been a little surprised that she did not have a Christmas present for him. He shrugged and placed it on the table. He had assumed perhaps with licence that she must have had a great affection for him when she asked him about his life. And now he sat in the chair glancing sideways, his head cocked to the right.

She looked behind him, to the waiting client outside and nodded, and Bines turned about and nodded also.

Then he turned back and looked at her.

"Jerry, I should tell you I'm involved."

"Involved – in what?" Jerry said.

"I mean I have a friend – he's studying Environmental Marine Biology in Halifax. Hadley and I are moving down in August if all goes well. He's second-generation Chinese Canadian – so he certainly knows about stereotyping."

She said this to prove that she knew other men with greater problems than Jerry Bines, problems that could in fact involve the court of world conscience.

"Environment – that there is what Ralphie is interested in. That there – environment."

"Yes," she said. She seemed distracted by this.

Bines looked at her and smiled.

"I knew that's what Ralphie is interested in," he said as if to please her.

There was a long silence.

"If we got our oil there – we'd perhaps be better off," he said. And then he added: "I was just wondering there if you want to go for coffee."

"Oh, I can't go now," she said. "I'm up to my chin in work."

"Up to yer chin," Bines said. But he did not know how to say anything else. He carried his left hand crooked against his side, and he was bleeding in his left lung, so that when he breathed his breath came short and pained.

Later on, Vera was to relate this episode to people on occasion.

She got to her feet first and started towards the door. And Bines stood and brushed against her. Then he bent over suddenly and kissed her, not on the mouth, but on the side of the face, roughly, and held her to him for a second, so her breasts flattened against his parka.

She drew back startled. A look of humiliation swept over her face, clouding her expression.

Bines stepped back and wiped his mouth.

"It was the most brutal thing I've ever experienced," Vera later said. "The least appreciative of the true nature of affection between a caring man and woman." But she felt she had to say this, and it was what others would expect her to say.

The boy's uncle maintained that none of the Pillars ever saw Bines again. But the other man stated that he was discounting the strangest event of all:

Ralphie was sleeping. Adele was curled up beside him. It was about 1:00 in the morning on December 17.

There was only the light of the street in the room. And a thaw had come, which had made the ground foggy. It rose over the trees and parted against a glassy sky. Lights from the street cast down feebly through the dark near the old schoolhouse.

Adele woke. To her dread she felt the presence of someone across the room on the far side of the window, sitting on the French chair in the corner by their blue coverlet. It was the dread of an apparition in a room late at night, like you have when you are a small child.

Bines was drinking a quart of wine. He seemed more happy to see them, than she was to see him.

It was as if he were a shadow from some other space and time, which had come back from the past, and was looking in upon a future where he did not belong, dismayed at being cast out and having to perform a task in order to rest. He was in darkness, so that his hands looked as if they were cast in the same mould as his jacket.

And like someone seeing an apparition, she was uncertain if he were there or if she were deluded by night terrors in the form of shadows playing upon the objects in a room.

Later she thought he had whispered something but she could never be certain. Everything had the vague substance of a dream, and when she woke up later it was morning, and a pale cold light slanted into the corner where he had been.

15

On the night of December 18 Rils insisted they go to Nevin's to get some money he'd heard about.

They went through the back streets and over a rickety fence. It was said later that Nevin woke up when the fence creaked – or he woke up shortly after that. No one knew who was in the room first.

It was after three in the morning. A small, sparse Christmas tree sat on the dresser, and outside the fog lay thick on the snow.

The thing that was remembered by Rils later, during his statement to police, was that when they came in, Nevin sat up and fumbled to put on his glasses and smiled suddenly.

"Did he know who you were?" the police asked.

"He must have," Rils said. "Or he knew who Jerry was."

"Did you know who he was?"

"I'd seen him at Lucy's one day. I heard he had money."

"And what did he say to you?"

"He didn't speak. He just looked at us as we went about the room. We were opening everything we could get our hands on – he didn't have much there."

"And this was at three in the morning?"

"This was after three in the morning, yes."

"What did Mr. White do?"

"Nothing," Rils said. "He just looked about as we worked – have you got a smoke?"

"Who had the shotgun?"

"I had the shotgun."

(At first Mr. Rils stated that Jerry had the shotgun.)

"You had the shotgun."

"I had the shotgun."

"Why didn't you like Mr. White?"

"I don't know. I just didn't like him – did not like that man."

As best as Mr. Rils could explain it, Mr. White was innocent, and he didn't like him. There was an innocence to his very nature that wasn't exactly good or bad. His innocence fell into a different category – it came from an unreasoned idea of his own importance: the importance of his socks, his shoes, his toothbrush.

"And this is what you didn't like."

"Something like that," Rils said.

"And Jerry said to him that you had come to borrow some money."

"That's what Jerry said, that I'd come to borrow some money."

"And what did Nevin do?"

"He only smiled and nodded – and said the only money he had was for his little girl."

"How much was in the tin box?"

"One hundred thirty-two dollars."

"That was all – there was no ten thousand dollars?"

"There was one hundred thirty-two dollars. I'd been told there was a lot more."

"By Jerry?" the police asked.

"No, not by Jerry."

"What did Nevin do then?"

"It was Jerry – Jerry wouldn't take the money –"

(In his first statement Mr. Rils suggested that it was he who didn't want to take the money.)

Rils stated that they turned on the light and Nevin was sitting up in the bed in his underwear. He was very thin, and he kept shaking his legs back and forth because he was cold, and he had red bumps on both knees. He had pictures of a girl all over his room, which Rils later found out were Hadley. Nevin coughed and began looking for a cigarette. He rolled one and told them that he hadn't had a drink in four days.

"Did he tell you or Jerry?"

"Pardon me now?"

"Did he tell you or Jerry this about his drinking – that he hadn't had a drink in four days?"

"Oh – I don't know – he told Jerry, and Jerry said: 'That's good then – that's good –'"

"And then what did Jerry say?"

"Jerry said he didn't want his money."

"And what did you say then – did you respond to that?"

"I said we'd take the money."

"And Jerry grabbed your hand."

"Well, he had a strong arm."

Rils said that Nevin also had a pack of loonies – about nine of them.

"He told you you could take those?"

"Yes, he did."

"What did he say when you threatened to tape the shotgun to his throat."

"I never did that."

"Well, you stated earlier that you did. You stated on January seventh that you had threatened to tape the shotgun."

"Oh, that. Nevin said he was sending the money to Hadley – and if we wanted money from him we would have to wait – he didn't seem scared anymore."

"That's when Jerry told you to leave."

"Yes – told me to leave."

"And that's when you decided to kill Jerry Bines."

Rils didn't answer this. He simply restated that they left the apartment intact, and took no money. That he was broke and cold and lonely and, not having been able to sell his jewellery, he felt it had been a wasted trip.

"Why did you hit Mr. White?"

"I wanted him to confess."

"To confess what?"

"To confess that he had a lot of money – everyone said he had a lot of money – all the street talk was that he had a lot of money – so I was surprised."

"Do you think Jerry was simply trying to keep you from robbing Ralphie Pillar?"

"I don't know."

"And what was Mr. Bines doing when you were hitting Mr. White?"

"He was looking out the window as if this had nothing to do with him. He seemed to have removed himself from it entirely."

(There were some questions asked about Nevin's ex-wife, Vera Pillar.)

"And what did Mr. White say?"

"He said he would not give the money to us because it was for his daughter. I never thought he would be brave."

"And that's when Jerry told you to stop hitting him?"

"I don't remember –"

"But on January seventh you stated that."

"Well, maybe – maybe not – I don't remember what Bines said most of the time."

The reasoning the boy followed was that Jerry was trying to save everyone. His reasoning was romantic. But, lying in bed at the cottage in mid-July, he would think it all over. Jerry hadn't wanted to steal the tractor-trailer, but he had been forced into it. (The boy did not know how Jerry had been forced into it, but he only reasoned he was.) After they had stolen it he refused to sell the cigarettes and a fight occurred over it between him and Buddy.

Then, to atone for Joe Walsh – the man who was his uncle – he made friends with Ralphie. To atone for his son he gave the wheelchairs, and tried to get his son to Halifax as soon as possible.

Andrew's uncle was far more cynical. He said that Bines knew Rils was coming, so he made friends with anyone he knew who would be able to give him an alibi – he made a big deal of everything so people would know about his boy. It was part of his histrionics. And he told his story to Vera, which was a way to impress her, about how he wanted to change.

"He worked like that there all his life," the boy's uncle said.

What the boy wanted to find out was about Buddy's death.

"Well, Jerry would use you whenever he could," his uncle said. "And he had Rils and Buddy steal the trailer – but then he got worried about it. There were too many ways to get caught. Bines liked to use people and cause trouble. It isn't right to steal – but all Buddy wanted was his money –"

The boy liked the other idea, that Jerry was protecting Joe Walsh.

Andrew's uncle wasn't fascinated by this at all.

"But it was Percy Rils Bines had to worry about," his uncle said. "You can't steal a tractor-trailer from an uncle who brought you up and have grand feelings –"

The man had another theory – that Jerry did not know who the tractor-trailer was going to be stolen from.

This is the theory that had surfaced in the last few months. That Jerry tried desperately to get Joe off the hook because Rita was ill. It seemed a nice thought to the boy.

His uncle countered this by saying that Jerry had a more perfect solution. Take no responsibility for it – pay no money for it, refuse to help move it, until Joe Walsh was charged with it, and they would be home free. If Buddy and Rils were caught he would not be implicated. And if Joe was charged, he could then manoeuvre about and be friends with Buddy and Rils once more, and make his estimated profit of thirty thousand dollars.

"The idea that Jerry was protecting someone like Joe is a good story – the truth is always somewhere else."

16

The place was never measured in any way. The scene was a redundancy of sharp broken trees cast into the naked sky, the earth cast up the thousands of acres clipped and broken, the roads twisting here and there, winding their way through what was previously dug up and rooted out. Far away the trail of smoke ebbed like a fingerling in the cold blue sky. His wife's house stood back from a road, naked and white with pink curtains in the upstairs window, as nondescript as a thousand other houses in the rural areas of the provinces.

On December 21 he went to get Amoxil for his son at a pharmacy in town. Then he took his presents over to Hazel and Lucy and Frances. He stayed thirty minutes to help adjust the outside Christmas lights for them and then he drove away.

He stopped at Sullivan's Groceries and bought some cookies, the kind his son liked.

He did not have the tree yet, so he must have gotten it between the time he left Sullivan's and the time he picked up Rils. He could have gotten it at the Irving five miles further on.

For some reason when he arrived at the house he had Gary Percy Rils with him. Again this was a glitch in his nature, something he had intended never to do, unless, as was said later, he had not judged Gary Percy well, or intended to kill him there and then.

His wife watched them from the small window in the living room as they got out of the truck. Everything was in slow motion. It was as if every step had been played over and over in her mind a thousand times before that, her wild man coming home to disrupt the house with a friend from his other life.

Jerry was not a good man, make no mistake. She remembered the night he had tied a noose to the kitchen beam and was going to hang a friend for saying something he didn't like. And he would have done it, too, of that there was no question in her mind, until she begged him to desist.

What was said was the thing said only in one of those arguments that happen when each of us is drunk, Bines later admitted. I might have been wrong to try and hang him, but he was wrong in saying what he said –

although, when I think of it, I was too drunk to remember what it was.

At first she had been naive enough to believe that he had never done anything, and dismissed all the times Constable Petrie came up to put him in cuffs. But slowly that changed. She saw how people would come to him and ask him his permission about who to rob.

He would nod his head slowly to one, say no to another, his voice so soft that it would be hard to believe it carried such power. "Don't burn *him* out," he would say to one. "No – that's no good – no good." Or, with his head turned slightly sideways, and his eyes cast down, he would nod, yes – and everything would be comprehensible.

She became more certain of this when Gary Percy Rils arrived in 1986, because over him Bines had no power.

As she watched them walking towards the house now, she saw that Gary Percy wore industrial leather mittens, soft shoes, and suit pants from some city somewhere. He was dressed in a patchwork of two different worlds. His face looked peaked because of a greying beard.

It seemed to her that things took forever, or happened in an instant.

Willie had run to the door to meet his father, but she grabbed him and said: "Shhh," and already she was trembling.

She remembered that she sat Willie on the bed in the

far room and closed the door, and when she turned around they were in the kitchen, the door still opened and the pale afternoon light sweeping in, with its smell of snow and winter dirt.

In retrospect the argument must have started in the truck about the Pillars. She did not know what it was about exactly. Gary following Bines about the room, and Bines, his eyes always on him, saying: "No – not taking you there – no," in a quiet voice.

The various prison psychiatric reports on both men suggested paranoid megalomania. All of this Vera eventually mentioned in her book. And it was one darkness pitted against the other, as Bines' little boy sat in the room, listening.

Jerry told Loretta that Rils would be leaving that day. Bines turned sideways and shut the door quietly. He took the shotgun from under his coat, and placed it on the kitchen table. Then he took the handle off and placed it on a chair, and took a small butt handle from his pocket.

But it didn't fit and he kept working at it. Gary went over and looked out the window. Some snow began to fall slowly down and made the earth white again.

"I'll fix this for ya, and then I'll drive ya out of town."

And on the radio came a song: "Oh come let us adore him. . . ."

He jammed the handle up and taped it with electrical tape, and held it in is hand to fashion the grip.

"Try this," Bines said, and he placed it on the table.

"I'd never be able to shoot," Gary said, picking it up, and looking disdainfully at it.

"Well, I'll put the other handle on, and take it like that," Jerry said.

"Too long."

"Then I'll cut it down."

They looked at each other. There was dead silence. After a long moment, Jerry said: "I'll cut it down."

"Saw it off at the front."

"No."

"Saw it off."

Jerry shrugged and looked at his work.

"It's okay," he said.

Gary said that Alvin might be able to do it, and they should go into town.

"No." Bines shrugged and stood up slowly, and it was at this moment that Loretta looked at Rils. His eyes were fixed on the distance, yet filled with an inner self-loathing that could be felt across a room.

"Tell him to stay where he is," Bines said to Loretta. "I'll bring the tree in." He was speaking of Willie, but Rils said he could go where he wanted. He seemed to become very agitated by this.

Bines looked at him. "Not talking to you," he said.

Mrs. Bines then stated that they were putting the tree up in the living room. This was the next thing she remembered about events. She did not remember Bines coming in with the tree, and the cookies under his arm.

He called to Willie to come out. "Got you your tree," he said.

The little boy looked at it, as little boys do, suddenly unfettered and released from the adults around him.

"Go get those tools for the stand," Jerry smiled. "The ones I give ya after I fixed yer wagon – fixed yer wagon –" He smiled at this too, and looked at his wife, for some reason hoping that she would be pleased.

Rils wanted to go, but Jerry told him there was time, and that he was putting up the tree, like he said he would.

"I don't like trees," Rils said. "I got things to do."

For some reason peculiar to his nature, he began to tease Willie. No one knew what this was about. "What do you think of your father?" Rils said.

Willie had come out of the room and was standing there with two screwdrivers in his hand. He wore his white cap, because his hair had not finished growing out. He looked up cautiously at his father when Rils spoke. Then he looked at Rils and said nothing.

"Like yer father – doncha, Will?" Jerry said. "Like your father."

"How do you like your father?" Rils said again. "If you don't like your father, join the club," Rils said. "Join the club – right Loretta – join the club."

"Not going to join any club, are ya, Will?" Jerry said softly, as if to smooth things over.

"Join the club," Rils said again.

Jerry glanced over at him but he was trying to put the

tree in the stand. And out of character, but because he was trying to impress Willie, he told his wife to tell Willie about the man in the Bible. "The one there who gives the lad all the clothes and food when he's in trouble," he said, and he glanced over at Rils.

"Oh, the Good Samaritan," Loretta said gently.

"Ya – the good lad there," Bines said. "Who hides the lad out and feeds him," he said, "even though no one else in the world will."

Willie looked cautiously about, at the man in the corner, and then suddenly smiled.

And Bines looked at him and smiled gently back. Then he turned away, as if in utter disdain and contempt for injury and began searching for the lights in the box of Christmas decorations.

"Now, when we get the tree up – we're going to invite some people up for supper –" Bines said.

"Gram," the boy said.

"Gram," Jerry said as if the boy had guessed it.

Rils went into the kitchen for a moment. Supposedly there was something said about the little boy's hair, and about wearing the white cap.

"His hair will come again," Jerry said. "Won't it, Will – what did the doctor say in Halifax – what did she say?"

"Hair will grow back," Willie said.

"That's what the doctors say at Ronald McDonald – right, Will?"

Willie was standing with icicles in his hand waiting to put them on the tree.

"You don't mind no hair anyway – do you, Will?"

Willie didn't answer.

"Anyone can have that old hair," Jerry said.

"The boy was standing with the icicles, and he turned to me to give me some," Loretta said in her statement to Constable Petrie. "I wasn't watching Mr. Rils. I had mentioned about supper the next evening and that perhaps Jerry and his grandmother could come over then. Jerry had just been called to go work a boat, and he didn't know if he could come. Although I knew he was too sick to work. He was moving very slowly – I was surprised. It depended on what shift, he said. I remember him being very agitated about this, because he had forgotten it, and he didn't want to disappoint the boy. It seemed to bother him more than things usually did. 'Well, I'll come up after work – no matter when,' he said, 'I'll be here.' I mentioned to him that he could phone someone to work for him, but he was displeased with this also. Now that I think of it, of course – he needed money for Christmas."

(Her statement continued after a question from Constable Petrie about a lock of hair encased in plastic and found in Jerry's shirt pocket. Loretta said she didn't know about it, and then answered a question about Rils)

"No, not at all. I don't think he was worrying about Mr. Rils at all."

(Her statement continued)

"Yes, he was short with Willie – because of the icicles, but I think he was thinking more about supper the next night. 'No,' he said. 'Go sit down until the lights are up,' is what he said. He said it more sharply than he ever said anything to William before. And I'm sad about this now."

(Her statement continued)

"No, William sat down and watched from the corner. I don't know what Mr. Rils was doing – except the argument they were having continued. Then I knew it was about seeing to Mr. White. Rils hated him – and he said he wanted to see about Mr. White."

(Her statement continued)

"Jerry said no. He didn't elaborate one way or the other. The other argument – over the phone, yes. Jerry didn't want Mr. Rils to use the phone because he thought there was a tap on it. Mr. Rils said he wanted to phone Calgary. But the argument only lasted a second because Jerry walked over and hauled the phone out of the wall and came back in."

(Her statement continued)

"No, Calgary. No, Buddy wasn't mentioned. I remember at one point Alvin was mentioned. No, the tractor-trailer wasn't. No, money wasn't mentioned at all. He didn't say if he was trying to get money from people in Calgary. I don't know why he wanted to phone Calgary. I thought it was because of Christmas."

(Her statement continued)

"No, as I said, I wasn't watching Mr. Rils. There was no liquor involved. No – I don't know – Jerry always had cocaine, so there could have been. He was in pain so he probably had cocaine."

(Her statement continued)

"I did not know anything about Mr. Rils wanting to do that – to the Pillars. I didn't know about the history of it. No, Jerry wanted nothing to do with it. He told him, no, he wouldn't take him into town, and I now assume he meant he wouldn't take him into town to go there and do that."

(Her statement continued)

"I don't know where Jerry was going to take him. I assume he wanted to get him out of town. He didn't like Mr. Rils – he never liked him. I don't know if he was scared of him – I know he didn't like him – and he tried not to argue with him, but Mr. Rils wanted to argue. I was upset over this because it was Christmas.

"Yes. I told the story about the Good Samaritan. I read it to Willie while he was sitting on the couch. There was a Bible in the kitchen but I didn't have to go in there. I have a small New Testament in a drawer in my living room. That's where I read it from.

"Yes. It did upset Mr. Rils to hear this. He thought Jerry was saying he was the Good Samaritan and Mr. Rils was the man beaten up. Mr. Rils then said that he was the Good Samaritan. 'A better Samaritan than you,' he said.

"A good Samaritan – no – I think Jerry at times might have been one – you see, what was given to him was not given to us and so he lost a chance most of us don't have. This is what I've come to think. I don't know what he thought of it at all really. Mr. Petrie – I was scared to death of him. And if a man thinks he is good simply because he doesn't kill you – then he is not – he's immoral.

"No. He was very angry about the tractor-trailer all that summer. He did not like what they had done to Joe Walsh, and he turned against them. He became cold, and then it didn't matter what happened.

"No, Adele nor Rita never spoke to him."

(Her statement continued)

"He spent a year with the Walshes, when he was five years old. This is what he told me. He always liked them. I think he used Joe – yes. I think Joe trusted him, took him to AA – because there was leniency with the parole board if Jerry did this. When I met him he wasn't drinking. No, I think he used Joe – and got to know his route and when he picked up cigarettes – and then they did it. Although with Jerry you are never sure.

"If any of us knew that Jerry had set it all up we chose not to believe."

(Her statement continued)

"No, because everyone has deceived people – I think, in little ways if not big ones."

(Her statement continued)

"Our house is sectioned in two. So Jerry's left side was turned to Mr. Rils, but he could not see him if Rils was in the kitchen – that's the only way I could explain it. He didn't see Mr. Rils. His left side was turned to him, and snow was falling, in the way snow falls suddenly, so you can't see anything outside. The marker at the end of our property line was blurred, and I remember thinking it was as if our world was cut off – and I became worried that there was no way to take the boy out if he got sick. But then I knew Jerry would – even if he had to carry him to town, and I relaxed when I thought this. No, there was no real chance of him getting sick that afternoon – I'm one of those people who exaggerate not how sick he is but how well he is, and so I continually tell people how well he is. Of course, his susceptibility to colds and infections worried me – but Jerry more. That's why he panicked when he took him to the hospital. It was a sad day for him. He did not know that the doctors were really as concerned as he was. He had bundled up the boy and took him there thinking that he could arrange everything. People like Jerry have some problem with ordinary life. If there was ruin in the nation he would smile and overcome it, but he had never graduated to the idea of being slighted.

"I knew there was going to be no benefit, but I knew he was trying to have one – and it could have been arranged. Everything would have turned out – if there had been time.

"Ralphie Pillar was good for him. He brought Jerry

out of himself. But change – no. Jerry would never change – that's why I left him."

There was a series of questions about this. About her leaving with the boy, about Jerry – about the court order – which at first she thought was necessary.

"Oh, Vera Pillar suggested it. She suggested I get the court order long before she ever met him. Jerry never knew this about her. And I did not dare tell him. But then when Jerry knew how sick the boy was, our feelings softened towards each other. At least, I think mine did. Of course, I always loved him – loved him? Yes, of course I did."

There was a question about Jerry's first wife – was this who Rils was trying to get in touch with in Calgary?

"I don't know anything about the woman – Trenda. You'd have to go back to his early life, which was not my time with him."

Loretta spoke of why Jerry did not go to the hospital. They found he had been bleeding slowly into his lung and that his left arm had been damaged. Loretta said it was because of Rils – he could not afford to leave Rils unattended.

(Her statement continued)

"Mr. Rils never touched the shotgun. This is what he was looking out for. Each time Jerry glanced into the kitchen he saw the shotgun where it was. He also believed that there was a .308 in the corner room – he did not know that I had given it away a year ago."

Loretta made very much of the music on the radio. Everything in the house was darkening, and the wind blew. The chairs took on a heaviness, the slanted doors became heavier. But the music had changed, and softened. It was Pachelbel's Canon, she later learned; she did not know this at the time. Why this music had suddenly come on the radio was because Mr. Rils had fiddled with the dial, and then gave it a twist and walked away from it. And faintly the sound of music entered the room, filling all the shades of darkness and light, the pink curtains turning in the twilight, and snow seeping and sifting along the outside of the windows and through the hard spruces at the property's edge. Everything was so still.

The air was still, and darkness coming, and music played, complementing the way classical music does complement the idea of parkas and toques and hands that have been battered most of their lives by work. Does complement the mills and the frost into the earth rather than the sophisticates who would snigger at a failed colleague in a room.

"Bines could not do otherwise with Mr. Rils. If he didn't bring him to the house Mr. Rils would have disappeared into town, to see to Mr. White or the Pillar family. In this way — if he had him at the house — he could keep an eye on him. To keep him from the Pillars — Ralphie and Vera. This is what I know now. He had to keep him in his sight.

"No, I did not know everything about the murder in Sudbury or the jewellery he had stolen, but I knew the police were looking for him because it had been in the paper and on television. So I knew who was with Jerry before he even got out of the truck."

(Her statement continued)

"Mr. Rils came back in. He sat down in the chair near the door. One moment he would look your way, and the next he would shift his eyes. Jerry was not paying attention to him at all. He had to run the extension cord to the socket, and he had asked me to go get an extra piece of cord. He was saying he might have to move the whole tree over but I wanted it near the window, and it was the same thing every year.

"No, Mr. Rils went and got the cord. He seemed fine. Jerry took the cord and thanked him. William kept saying, 'The lights, Mom – the lights,' so I said, 'Okay, open the icicles if you want.' William looks younger than he is, and he speaks slowly. He started to hand me the box of icicles to open it for him, and Jerry said, 'Oh, the Amoxil.' He had it in his pocket and it has to be refrigerated. He had forgotten all about it probably. He turned to William and started to reach in his pocket.

"'Take this to the fridge – out to the fridge,' I heard him say distinctly, and then he cast a glance to his left. Everything seems to be in slow motion now. He cast a glance as if he were curious why Mr. Rils had jumped up. And I could tell he was about to turn and smile.

"And Mr. Rils stabbed him, under the parka and into

his left side. Willie didn't see it – he had his hands on the box of icicles – and he looked over at his father because Jerry had uttered a sound. It was as if his breath was cut off.

"Jerry swung his right arm around in back of him and broke Mr. Rils' jaw. But then he stumbled. Mr. Rils fell back against the wall, and Jerry tried to pull out the knife. 'Pull it out,' he said to me. 'Pull it out.'"

(Her statement continued)

"Yes, I did. I went over and pulled the knife out. Mr. Rils was in the kitchen, trying to put the shotgun together. Jerry fell over against the tree. It seemed like a long time. He tried to get up and fell again. Willie tried to help him up, and I had my hands under his arms.

"'Take Willie out the back porch – back porch, take him over to Donovan's,' he said. 'Take him over to Donovan's, Loretta –' he said.

"I took Willie and ran into the back porch, but I didn't go out, I opened the hatch and went into the cellar. I told Willie to hide."

(Here there was a series of questions about the shotgun. Loretta's statement continued)

"He hid behind a box with a few icicles still in his hand, and you could see his feet sticking out. When I started upstairs he looked up over the box at me. 'Get down,' I said.

"Oh yes, yes, yes. Jerry knew Mr. Rils would kill the boy – and me, too. What else would he do? We all know now about Mr. Rils. But I didn't think of that then.

When I came upstairs the music was playing, and I remembered that the lights had come on out in the road.

"I didn't see Jerry when I went into the room. But I could see Gary Percy making his way into the snow. He was just on the far side of the truck."

(There was a question from Constable Petrie about what Jerry was doing, where he was, and what, if anything, he said)

"He was slumped down by the fridge. He had wrestled the shotgun out of Rils' hand and was trying to put it together. There were shotgun shells all over the place. What did he say? He told me to put the Amoxil in the fridge and get the .308. I told him I had given it away.

"There was blood all down the side of the fridge and against the wall.

"I put the Amoxil in the fridge. He was no longer strong enough to open the shotgun and put a shell in it. I asked him if he wanted a priest, because he was baptized a Catholic. I went to telephone the hospital – I know the number off by heart – but Jerry had torn the phone from the wall."

(There was a question from Constable Petrie if Jerry wanted a priest)

"No."

(There was a question from Constable Petrie about Rils coming back to the house)

"No. The next thing I knew the police had picked him up in Jerry's truck at the train station in Moncton."

(There was a question from Constable Petrie asking if Jerry was alive when Mr. Donovan got across the road)

"No."

"He was not alive when Mr. Donovan came in?"

"No – he was not alive – Jerry was not alive at that time."

17

A month after Jerry's death, the two ministers of Loretta Bines' church, a father and son who looked identical (each weighed over two hundred pounds, and wore identical suits, and the boy had his hair dyed to look like his father's), came one day to the house to visit, and ate pies and cakes sitting in the living room in mid-afternoon.

Each looked very canoned, ministerial, as the cold snow froze in the puddles, and their cars, both Buick Regals, were pulled up bumper to bumper in the little drive outside her house. Each wore leather shoes that were pointed to make them look like they only had a couple of toes on each foot, each wore the same gold jewellery – watches and rings. Each was constantly offended. Each spoke about the French, and taxes, and Catholics, and Bible school, and their summer camp.

"Brother Bob and his boy Teddy," people called them.

They had a trailer park, and a mobile home for sale, and they expected Loretta to clean it. In fact, they never came over until they needed her to scrub or clean the church, or help in their trailer park.

This afternoon they were here to drive her to the church because the cross was going to be put up. It was far away, across two broken roads in a community which had been cut out of the earth just two years before.

In the sky the clouds were grey and light, and the day seemed to stand still. The snow about the churchyard had frozen to ice and the ice had the same tone as the sky, flat and off-white with strands of yellow.

The deer had come out to the frozen stream below the church, into the small pasture, and young pastor Teddy tried to shoot one, following it around the pasture in his suit and holding the .308 rifle that he had borrowed from Loretta last year. The small group of men and women watched him do this – the men exclaiming that if he fired now the deer would be history.

But then the deer bounded over a few falls and crossed the river, and, like deer do, jumped in splendid retreat against the old spruce woods, so that one moment it was gone and the next they saw it palavering in the crooked shadows of the lonesome tangles.

Teddy walked back, hiding the gun under his suit, for hunting season was long over, his pointed shoes soaking, and saying that deer could run like the devil when they saw a pastor, and everyone laughed.

"I had my hopes pinned on you, Young Teddy," one of the men said.

He smiled at this and handed the rifle to someone, as if not being so good with the rifle meant nothing to him personally, and then he looked up at the works above the church – the high scaffolding and the cross leaning against the door.

They all stood about wondering who would put the cross up and one of the children, a sixteen-year-old boy with a ready smile, started to climb the ladder.

He stood on the scaffolding and looked down and waved.

Loretta was standing with the small group of women.

Pastor Bob stood back against the door, not speaking. It was a certain kind of apoplexy came over him when things had to be done. He'd simply wait and others would look at him and shout: "Get it done for Bob."

This became the expression of their humanity now in the grave little yard in the middle of the afternoon.

"Get it done for BOB!"

Two men lifted the cross, and tied a rope to it, and the boy began to haul. It banged its way up, and was caught in the scaffolding rods.

The deer came again to the field below and walked unconcerned against the scrapes left two months before.

One of the men who lifted the cross was Nevin White.

He had met the ministers two weeks before, and now, leaning on the scaffolding, his hair cut short, his old suit on, faded almost to nothing, he looked like most of the others.

They had promised him a new life. And it was in this new life that he put his hope.

"Can you help a man who attempted suicide and beat a child – and tormented his first wife?" he had asked them (for he'd always believed he'd beaten a child when he had only teased one).

"Of course," they had said.

And he was startled, like Nevin always was, when confronted with simplicity or action.

It was in this new life where he hoped to find his self-respect, and to forgive himself the memory of his first wife.

He had told Vera where he was. "I'm going back to church," he had told her.

"Yes," Vera said. "Of course you are – well, good for you."

"I haven't had a drink in four weeks," he had told her. "And I'm going to get a job – it won't be much of a job – but it will do."

"Well – good for you," she said.

It was very strange that this would happen to him. It was very strange that in a way he was doing what he felt he must do, even though the whole world – almost all of his friends, and certainly all of those down to a man or woman he wanted to impress – would now turn away.

He shivered in the cold, and wisps of grey snow began to fall out of the sky, and then run to water as they hit his cheeks.

The little group, all dishevelled men and women, outcasts in every way, looked at each other. Not one was a carpenter, not one a mechanic, not one was a professional. All of them had dismal records of failure and loss. But they had taken to building this church by themselves.

And Nevin looking around at them suddenly smiled. His skin was so white it looked like ivory, and his hair cut was in the fashion of a Roundhead from the seventeenth-century civil war. He climbed the scaffolding with two others.

"Hand it to me," he said. "Hand it to me."

He did not know why he said this. Certainly in his former life he had done nothing like this.

"Hand it to me," he said again.

The pastor opened his hymn book and walked back and forth, for no other reason than he thought that this was what he should be seen to be doing, the pages spattered with snow, which somehow impressed him, the old gouged earth red with rigid muck under his feet.

Nevin looked down.

No one knew him, and he knew none of them.

When he had brought his books to the rented trailer – a most quixotic collection of books – sex manuals sat atop the environmental study of 1987, atop works by Schopenhauer and Kant near cookbooks and Andy Capp comic books – the young minister had smiled at him ruefully and had said: "You won't need none of those here."

"Oh," Nevin said.

"You'll find there is only one work here – the work of the Lord."

At the second tier of the scaffolding Nevin was the first to touch the cross and it was ice-cold on his hands. He lifted it, with the help of a grey-haired man, who, still bending over, began to teeter as if he might fall headlong into the muck below.

But Nevin balanced him and lifted the cross from him.

"I got it," he said.

The sixteen-year-old with a heavy accent from upriver shouted: "We got her right there now."

The scaffolding went up another two tiers and then

only one person could place the cross into the wooden support and bolt it.

"Put it on me back and I can climb right up there," the grey-haired man said.

"I'll help," Nevin said.

"Mr. White," someone shouted from below, "your pants are unhooked."

And Nevin saw that his pants were unhooked from the cross scraping against them, and he smiled.

"Yes," he said, and he hooked his pants again and tightened his belt.

The wind suddenly blew against him, and held him back against the steeple.

"Tie the rope – tie a rope on," the same man shouted to the grey-haired man, looking not at him but at one of the pastors.

"It's all right," Nevin shouted. "We'll jimmy it up."

And he went up to the next tier – battered by wind and cold snow, the little group of people huddled below watching him as he dragged their cross behind him.

But he was not all right at all. He was scared to death and he did not know why he was doing such a foolish thing.

The boy stood beneath him on a small platform with his hand on the bottom of the cross, and when he let go the cross swayed in the wind and Nevin grabbed it with both hands, and almost fell between the scaffolding and the steeple.

Some people shouted out to him to be careful.

But Nevin and the boy and the older man managed to get the cross to the last tier. The older man sat down on the scaffolding to catch his breath.

"Come up to the walkway," Nevin said to the boy, "and we'll put it in together."

The walkway was only a foot and a half wide, and the scaffold had ended. They could reach down and brace themselves at the top, but only if they let go of the cross.

"It's heavy," the boy said, but still he had the same kind grin on his face, and he reminded Nevin of the child he had teased so many years before. Already he seemed to be much stronger than Nevin and he realized this.

"Give it to me," he said. "I'll place her there."

Nevin's face was cut and his hands were torn. He bled from every knuckle. "I'll do it," he said, "if you support my back."

"I'll come up," the old man said.

"No," the boy said. "There isn't room – you support our feet."

Far away they could see the river turn bleak into the sunless sky, and the trees distant and dark.

Nevin thought about Hadley – but she seemed far away from him. He had been angry with her, for hiding behind a chair in the living room when he went to pick her up on certain Saturdays, while Vera said: "Well, you have to go – it's your father."

But at this moment it didn't seem important.

The boy held on to him. The old man tried to support their ankles, and Nevin took the cross and lifted it into the socket. When it dropped into place he felt his hand jam and he winced.

"Hurray," two people called up. "You got it, Mr. White."

He climbed down from the scaffolding. People had drifted inside where there was to be a church service, and Nevin felt uncomfortable with this, so he stood outside the door. As he stood there his left hand bled, red blood dropping into the snow.

He was alone in the little churchyard. Suddenly he was depressed as he was at times when he thought of ending his life.

He thought of reading Kant in his studies at university and felt he had made a great mistake being here.

"Come inside," a woman said to him. He blinked and put on his glasses and looked at her. She was standing with her little boy near the door.

"Come on – you'll freeze yer arse off out there," she said. She smiled and he smiled also.

She was Loretta Bines.

He looked up at the cross. Now that it was done it didn't seem at all an important thing to do.

"You were brave to do that," she said. The little boy nodded and smiled at him.

He looked at her, and he felt he could easily mistake her for his first wife.

"I'm sorry, I'm so sorry," he said. "I've been a coward all my life. I'm sorry."

"Well, we're all as brave as we have to be," Loretta said, "and none of us are any braver."

"Forgive me," he said, his lips trembling, "forgive me."

But she only smiled kindly at him, and he could think of nothing more to say.

18

The word went out and Ralphie walked the streets from door to door to solicit support for a benefit for a boy hardly anyone knew. And yet the place was filled, and people were turned away at the door. A thousand people called to be tested for bone marrow. Yet the one who matched was the fifth person they tested – Adele Pillar. So she and Ralphie would visit Willie every week.

Their own daughter was sixteen years old, and very shy. She did not know them very well. But she still visited Adele and Ralphie now and again – although she found that Adele could not help bossing her and she empathized with her Aunt Milly much more.

Ralphie's hair went almost completely white over the

next few months. He wore ludicrous bow-ties and talked about things no one seemed to understand. He gave a talk at the high school comparing calculus and reductive biology, and an approach to it by modern man. Four people showed up. Adele's sister Milly and Adele and Ralphie's old high-school chemistry teacher and an old man no one knew. The old man looked baffled and said: "My God, boy, that's the most boring talk I've ever heard." And Ralphie had to agree.

He decided that spring that he might go back and do his Master's and he went over to visit his professor in physics, who, years ago, had told him he was the brightest student he had ever had.

But when Ralphie saw him he realized that the professor no longer knew who he was and then to make it worse he pretended he did. So Ralphie decided to go back to his shop. And he never spoke of it again.

Some time in April Adele received a phone call from a lady at the local bookstore. She did not know who else to call. So Adele went down. There in a big glossy edition was the book on dinosaurs Jerry had ordered for his boy.

Adele paid for the book, and said she would give it to William.

She saw Vera's book on a shelf near the door and glanced at it, but she never bought it. Something about it made her think of it as wounding someone in the heart, hunting someone who was wounded down.

Ralphie and she planted a garden that spring, and

that summer, in early July, they adopted a child. The feasibility study didn't matter anymore.

Vera stayed in town that summer to finalize her affairs, and sell the house, before moving with Hadley to Halifax, where Vera said there was so much work to be done.

When Vera left, Adele felt that part of her life was over forever. And a new life, whatever it was to be, with her husband and her adopted child had come. There was a sadness at the drive of the house when Vera came up to say goodbye. She glanced at Adele, and they both smiled timidly.

"You eat some – and get some weight on you," Adele said, as bossy as always, trying to hide her absolute love for people by being sharp.

"Take care of Ralphie," Vera whispered. "He would be lost without you."

The day of Jerry's death Alvin had decided to turn Jerry and Rils in for the reward. He sat in the station and he kept reaching over to shake Constable Petrie's hand. Later he blamed his wife and children for what he had done.

The following fall Lucy went to Moncton to take a course. No one knew who she was or how close to Mr.

Bines she had been. She never spoke about him, although there was a book and even talk about a movie. She had a wistful faraway look, and the wind blew in her dark blond hair.

She bought herself a little car. The kind that Buddy had always wanted. Coming home for Easter in late March she lost control of it and was killed just south of Rogersville. Adele and Ralphie paid for the funeral expenses.

Trenda, Jerry's first wife, made inquiries into his property – and certain benefits she might obtain.

Those who accused Joe Walsh of being implicated in the theft of the tractor-trailer still did.

19

Andrew learned of all of this over a length of time and pieced it together little by little. Some things he learned from overhearing his mother and uncle, some from the man who came those July mornings and took them to the cottage.

When Jerry was in prison, the man said, he'd taken a hot iron and burned the bare chest of another prisoner who was "making indecencies" towards him, so that the mark of the iron would always be visible on his chest, and it would always seem that he had pressed his shirt while wearing it.

Andrew had heard this at the cottage. He would listen to the old alarm clock ticking away in his mother's bedroom, the trees waving softly at night, a smell of perfume from the shrubs and flowers coming in through the screen door, and a mosquito as big as a truck continually bothering him.

The only time the boy had ever spoken to Bines was that night at the camp. Andrew had a scout knife and he wanted to show it to him, simply because he had shown it to everyone else.

Bines had been sitting in a chair in the far corner of the room. He had the peculiar habit of putting his head down and slightly away from a person as they spoke, but when the boy asked him if he would like to see his knife Bines looked up. His eyes, bolt-black as they were, seemed to be filled with a particular kind of light.

"Sure," Jerry said. And the boy brought his knife over to him. Jerry looked at it a moment. "Boy Scout, now," he said. "Boy Scout, are ya?" Then he handed the knife back.

The boy took the knife and then said: "But you haven't even seen all its parts – it has a whole bunch of different parts."

"Don't be saucy," the boy's uncle said quietly.

"No, no – let's see – see there," Jerry said, as if he didn't want to be rude. He took the knife in his hand and opened it.

"Got a spoon here," Jerry said, "and a pair of scissors – pair of scissors." And he reached over with the small pair of scissors and clipped a strand of hair from the boy's head, so that all the men laughed.

"There you go – I got your strand of hair –" And he took it and put it in his shirt pocket. "Next to my heart," Jerry said, smiling. "Keep it here next to my heart." Then he said: "You come back and get it from me when you're seventy. It'll still be here – next to my heart."

That night at the camp the boy thought that he would get his strand of hair back in about sixty years, if all went well, and he would take a piece of tape and tape it exactly back on the spot where Bines had cut it. He knew enough not to mention the hair again because that would lessen its importance.

And he had forgotten about it until this hot July evening. Half asleep, and sitting up in bed to take a round-house at the mosquito, he suddenly thought of the piece of hair.

Falling asleep he wondered what he would be doing at seventy.

Martin Flewwelling

David Adams Richards was born in Newcastle, New Brunswick, in 1950. He has published nine acclaimed novels, including the award-winning Miramichi trilogy – *Nights Below Station Street*, winner of the 1988 Governor General's Award; *Evening Snow Will Bring Such Peace* (1990), winner of the Canadian Authors Association Award; and *For Those Who Hunt the Wounded Down* (1993), winner of the Thomas Raddall Award – *Hope in the Desperate Hour* (1996), and *The Bay of Love and Sorrows* (1998). In 1993, Richards received the Canada-Australia Prize.

He has also published three non-fiction books, most recently the Governor General's Award-winning fishing memoir *Lines on the Water* (1998), and has written Gemini Award-winning screenplays for the CBC-TV adaptations of his novels *For Those Who Hunt the Wounded Down* and *Nights Below Station Street*. "Small Gifts," his original screenplay for CBC-TV, won a Gemini Award and the New York International Film Festival Award for Best Script.

Richards now lives in Toronto with his wife, Peggy, and their two sons. He is completing an original screenplay for a feature film. His new novel, *Mercy Among the Children*, was published in September 2000.